SAINTS
and
RUNNERS

OTHER BOOKS BY LIBBY SCHEIER

SKY— A Poem in Four Pieces
Language in Her Eye (Co-editor)
Second Nature
The Larger Life

SAINTS
and
RUNNERS

STORIES *and a* NOVELLA

by Libby Scheier .

Libby Scheier

for Francine —
enjoying the sensibility
you bring to class
Best

The Mercury Press

Libby
Aug 1/95
Toronto

ACKNOWLEDGEMENTS
"Letters to the Family" appeared in *Descant*. "Foreplay to Love" appeared in
Paragraph. "The Saint Who Frequented Prostitutes" appeared in *Prairie Fire*.
"Pretty Goldfish" appeared in *Canadian Woman Studies* and in the fiction
anthology, *Frictions*. "Brian's Dream/Arla's Fantasy" appeared in *NOW* as
"Donald's Dream" and in the fiction anthology *Love and Hunger*.

Many thanks to: my editor, Beverley Daurio; Victoria Freeman, George Galt, and
Phil Hall for reading and commenting on the draft; Ann Decter and Makeda
Silvera for commenting on a section of the draft; and two young, talented writers,
Jennifer Duncan and Sheri Katz, for reading and commenting on the draft and for
overall editorial assistance.
Thank you to the Canada Council for a B grant and a project grant, and to the
Ontario Arts Council for a Works-in-Progress grant.
My gratitude and love to my son Jacob and my family of friends (Henry, Ellie,
and Judith) for all their support, and for everything else, too.
§
The publisher gratefully acknowledges the financial assistance of the Canada
Council, the Ontario Arts Council, and the Ontario Publishing Centre.

Cover design by TASK/Ted Glaszewski
Composed in Bembo
Printed and bound in Canada by Metropole Litho
Printed on acid-free paper

First Printing, September 1993
1 2 3 4 5   97 96 95 94 93

CANADIAN CATALOGUING IN PUBLICATION DATA:
Scheier, Libby
Saints and runners
ISBN 1-55128-004-3
I. Title.
PS8587.C54S35 1993   C813'.54   C93-094759-2
PR9199.3.S35S35 1993

Represented in Canada by the Literary Press Group
Distributed in Canada by General Publishing
and in the United States by Inland Book Company (selected titles)

The Mercury Press
137 Birmingham Street
Stratford, Ontario
Canada N5A 2T1

For my dear friend, Henry King

CONTENTS

*IN*VITATION

I ONCE HAD A DREAM that everything I touched was covered by a film of warm sticky bubble gum, pale pink like my flesh, and I could not separate myself, my body, mind, whatever it is that I am, from any other object in the site of being I wandered through. Long pink strands stretched behind me, still attached to the objects I had come in contact with. Thin rubbery strings connected my fingers to the earth, and my arms hung down at my sides, drifting in my wake, palms of my hands facing backward like an ape's.

Dreams, facts, stories. One thing I like about writing is that I don't have to figure out which is which. Just let the truths and lies, the accuracies and the misses all jumble

9

together like they do in dreams, where they sparkle in the equality of ridiculous imagery.

I am addicted to story telling, to fashioning commodities out of the chaos of my existence here. Packaging *objets d'art,* bric-a-brac, *chachkas*—and offering them to you. It is a way to make sense out of the senseless, or, if there is no sense to be made, it is a way to create something you might use.

I speak to you from inside the unholy vessel of my body, from within my ribcage where my beating heart, pink and grey and sticky like gum, chafes against my sternum, trying to get out, trying to connect with the agents of its growth and destruction. The grey folds of my brain undulate like ocean. I speak from this place which is me, and these stories contain the truths of my recent living. But they contain lies, too. Because I find plot useful to protect myself from your unwanted intrusions into my life. It's unfair to speak of "intrusions" when I am *offering* you these things, I know. Yet it's how I feel. I suppose I wish to control the reader, a hopeless task, and yet one that seduces me.

There are things here I have made up to keep from you other things. My secrets. I like the way plot is suited to falsification. When I want to brazenly assert actual facts, despite their current unfashionability, I'll tell you.

I still do make that distinction, sometimes anyway, between fact and fiction. With discretion, meaning wise choice. Although I do acknowledge a large grey area.

Willy-nilly. Whether I like it or not. Sometimes I do and sometimes I don't. Like it. But the large grey area exists—a fact, in its own way. It is here that I invite you into the book I have organized, into the grey fields stretching into the distance ahead of us and behind, moving endlessly outward on either side of us. I invite you into the story here, so that you can twist and turn it to your liking. So that you can use it.

SAINTS
and
RUNNERS

LETTERS *to the* FAMILY

White Spider

RAINING A SLOW NIGHT RAIN on cultivated herbs and dense weed patches. Small garden off the laneway. Solemn erratic Scriabin on the stereo, beaten down by excessive virtuosity: the young pianist has career aspirations.

Dear Mother, I haven't been in love since I left Joe four years ago, and I don't know if I'm glad or sorry. I miss the way his love filled me with dense matter, how I could feel each step I took and how I never confused north from south, driving my car. But I don't miss sliding down the oily black hole of my love for him, the dark and odourless place of no top or bottom. Please advise.

scaling the far wall

a white spider

tiny albino eyeball
with outstretched veins

the hand of my grandmother
delicate and deliberate

pale flame

Dear Dad, What do men want? What if it's not what I want? It's not what I want. Please advise.

Hydro wires slice the wind, making me think of a dead poet who tried to become an organisation creature. Sharon Stevenson was a Maoist; her father was pro-Soviet. Mr. Stevenson attributed Sharon's suicide to Maoism, Marcusianism, and petty-bourgeois feminism. I'm not making this up. It's a direct quote and was printed in the *Toronto Star*, April 29, 1984. Dear Mr. Stevenson, Would you please reconsider your views? My personal optimism feels threatened. Respectfully. P.S. What do parents want?

I focussed on my face in the mirror this morning, studying new lines, the little ones crossing the border between the pink pubic-skin of my upper lip and the slightly fuzzy place below my nose and remembered a poem I wrote ten years ago about my mother's lipstick, how it crept up those lines, how make-up fails as camouflage. The image I used was: lipstick like little rivers of blood. Sign language of skin drying, saying, underneath is a human in physical decline.

Dear Sam, What do children want? Do they get it? Do you? Please advise. Love.

flutter of bird wings
gentle misfortunes   moments of grace
candles on the heads of bears

singing
in a green and mossy cave

waiting for waiting for
morning

Mark: What are brothers for? Please write.

Potted Plant

Monkeys sit in the laneway, eyes gleaming in the hot sunlight.
    It's summer again, Mother, and the daisy petals are the colour of your hair. How is Dad and why doesn't he write? The weeds in the garden are tall and waving in the hot breeze. All my friends are having late babies, learning how to pronounce "amniocentesis." No one has the courage to forego immortality, rushing to get pregnant before they turn 40. Maybe it's not immortality they're after, but ties that are less fragile. Building a family around them. They're all statistics—their own early departures from their parents' homes, the break-ups of their first marriages/cohabitations. Suddenly they discover there's no phoenix rising from the ashes. So it's back to the biology we all know.
    I try to write poems without people in them, but fail. My desire is for the calmness of stone, my habit the commotion of cells. I want to grow what I need inside me, water it like a potted plant, talk to it, and keep it secret. I'm sorry, Mother, about Dad's pain, and about your fears when you're alone. One of my students in the adult education class told me that being 70 is easier than being 35. Is that true?

Eyeballs

Dear Mark, Having an older brother is considered an exalted state by some teenage girls. And it was. We were so close in our early twenties we were almost lovers. Allies against Dad. But you succumbed to his steady grinding away and I didn't. Leaving helped. You stayed close to home and got more like him.

In high school I was the bright student who got the scholarship, became the working-class token at a fancy women's college. You muddled along; I was the family star. But I stayed a misfit, scraping by, failing at marriage. You got a wife, a house, and after 15 years, still have the same respectable job. You're the star now, Mark.

During the worst period of my life, you turned your back on me. That hurt worse than losing Joe. I'd loved you longer.

So you're 40 and I'm pushing and you're talking to me about "reconstructing" our relationship. And I ask myself: how the fuck did we get here, really? Of course I've got it all figured out and blamed on you, and I know you have done the same to me. But I don't want to be drenched through the eyeballs with this stuff, with Dad in and out of the hospital.

Bottles and Streets

Grey, humid pollution days. July. Sam is four this summer, Mother, and has started an independent social life. Kids come knocking at the door for him, and he goes off. I'm embarrassed to admit how ambivalent I feel about it. I'm proud to see he's growing up well, getting along with other kids, even that he's popular (which doesn't run in the family). But my first reaction was to be traumatized. About my baby growing up, of course. Something else to lose. Then in typical fashion, feelings of shame for being selfish. Finally, relief and pride when he doesn't come home beaten up and when the neighbourhood kids hang out on our porch, waiting for him to come out and play after dinner.

He keeps me dizzy, alternating sharp new feelings of independence with baby-like regression. Every day he picks a fight with me over my dictum that he can't cross the street by himself. It's the first running argument we've had and I can hear you say it won't be the last. Yesterday Sam requested the bottle again and sat in my lap playing baby, drinking it. Then, he began an argument with me about crossing the street, taking time out to suck at the bottle.

This must be how we all drive each other crazy over the years. Holding tight and pushing away. Holding tight and pushing away.

Rings

This room is so white and so high up in the air. I'm all alone. For a whole week. A room at the Holiday Inn combines the virtues of a bank vault and a lobby. Its sterility is perfect for me. Completely undistracting. The steady drone of downtown traffic is calming, a high-tech *OM*, a protective sound barrier hiding me from anyone who might know me, want something from me. The boring sameness of everything here is relaxing. Had to get away from the kid, house, garden, spiders on the wall. Even Scriabin was getting on my nerves.

I should write a letter to Joe. Dear Joe. Dear Father of My Child. Dear Love of My Life. Dear Disaster. That's what my mother would write. Dear Disaster. My father might say, Dear Rotten Husband of My Daughter and Irresponsible Father of My Grandchild. And my kid would say: Dear Dad, When are you coming? I want you to come soon.

Sam, of course, does not remember Joe. He was only a few months old when the marriage ended and Joe went back to Australia. But he has pictures of him and stories of him. He is madly in love with him.

Three lovers later, I'm still in love with Joe. In a way. A smaller way than before. The tree grows rings. My love for him is smaller, in relation to the rest of the rings, than it used to be. But it's there and will be. I'm glad I've got it inside me where it can't get out.

I'm looking forward to his visit in September. Even with his new wife. But I'm afraid. Not of being jealous, or of how Sam will behave. Afraid I'll find I don't love him any more. I like the idea of rings. I want to be right.

Dear Joe, I wanted to write a story about you but didn't know what to say. Instead, here are some drawings I've done of groups of people in which you appear as a character. They are about mental interactions between individuals—missed, failed, and successful. Let me know what you think of them. Best regards.

I'm drawing more these days, writing less. Painting more, too. Words frustrate me. They don't mean what I mean. Pictures, paint, lines, shapes—it's more complex, it's more things-all-at-the-same-time, more confused. More like life.

Rumania

I had an out-of-body experience before it was trendy. It was 10 years ago, at my grandfather's funeral, a perfect place for transcending the physical. A group of 20 or 30 of us approached the family plot. I saw my name on a gravestone and the jolt went through me from head to feet. I looked again and saw it was my grandmother's name. Anna. Almost mine. Arla. I'm named after her.

My spirit rose slowly in the air, about 30 feet, and I looked down at myself and my relatives. My grandmother made contact with me. She didn't have anything to say, she just let me feel her presence. She felt like rotting potatoes in Rumania. A strong Jewish peasant hiding in a basement from raping and murdering Germans. Holding my father's mouth so he wouldn't cry out and give her away. The other four kids crouching around her. Her husband gone already, two years before, to North America, preparing their new life. Seven years later the rest of the family came here and grew up poor. She was known as a tough, immoveable woman. Everyone was afraid of her. But her children were loyal to her, more loyal than to husbands and wives or anyone.

Do you want to come back, grandmother, just for a while, and say hello to everyone? No, I've had enough of all that. Now I am a witch among witches and do what I want.

Bull

You're the hardest person to write to, Dad. I'm in a panic because you're ill. I want to get it resolved between us, but don't know how.

We've always been so similar, so like grandmother,

we could never get along. We stand against each other, your backbone against mine, pillars of the continuing war between the sexes.

I visited a friend who's dying, the other day. I don't want to go back, but I will. I don't want to be distracted from the onset of my mid-life crisis by dying friends. Besides, she's too young to die and I don't know where to locate this in my jigsaw puzzle of people and scenes.

We'll have a good visit when I come in August. Not a big blow-up like last time. I'm sorry for yelling at you that you filled my head with "radical shit."

But why did you have to be so narrow-minded and dogmatic? Only your exact viewpoint has ever been the right one—for you and for everyone else. And the trouble with your viewpoint was that it was always so exact, so specific. No room for me to maneuver. It was either swallow everything you had to say, or confront the whole thing head on, like a crazed bull. And that is how I learned to become a crazed bull. I grew up in the spirit of combat. Compromise and tolerance were ideas I learned later.

And here's something else I hold against you. The way you sat on Mother's head all her life. The way you turned Mark into your creature and he turned against me.

See, I started out this letter saying I wanted to resolve the differences between us and I wind up setting my horns against you. How do I learn to put all this to rest?

White

The whiteness of the walls. And the heat, drifting 10 stories up from the pavement. The mornings are so uneventful here. Like riding on an empty subway train. Nothing to look at, and the steady mechanical hum of motor vehicles, white noise. White walls, white typing paper, white days. But my nights have been packed densely with long dreams, full of everyone I've known and everyone I haven't. It's as though the population of the world has come home to roost, home to the site of their invention, back to the scene of the crime, demanding that I justify my plots and characterizations, and come up with better endings, too. I wake up every morning with a headache, my body heavy with protagonists and scenarios jumbled together like a cutting room floor after a film editor's nervous breakdown. I don't dream like this at home. The demands of every day make me dream about what I have to do tomorrow. I dream lists: one, two, three, four—four things to do in the morning, six in the afternoon, and five phone calls in the evening. But I see monkeys in the laneway, and myself singing in a cave. Night dreams driven into daylight.

Dear Arla, It's too bad you have only a week here at the Holiday Inn. You need more time to dream things out.

There's always a fascination with being high up. The access to easy violence to the self is provocative. It makes you think more clearly, it has spiritual dimensions.

All my life, this was something other people did, thought about. It wasn't in my vocabulary. Until I had my child and my marriage came apart, all at the same time. I knew if I were patient enough I would feel better. But each day was three weeks long. I felt like I'd been given a 30-year prison sentence and didn't know if I could wait it out.

I did, and I felt better. But it stays with me. The tree grows rings. The option of self-destruction is something I return to every so often, to think about, to reject.

The moment of self-destruction is tantalizing, the aftermath less promising. The whiteness of walls, the heat, the steady white drone of motor vehicles.

Pictures

Some relatives say Sam looks like you, Mark. But it's only in the eyes, turned down at the outside corners, a little sleepiness and sadness always around the eyes. He'll be slim and tall like Joe. But he really looks like me. He'd better look like me, after all that work.

His turned-down eyes come at me sometimes, airborne snapshots. I'm back home after my week at the Holiday Inn, going through a box of old photos. Still haven't gotten an album for them. We all have something of each other, some intonation of expression, way of standing, that gets called family resemblance. But mainly each figure stands alone, individual, the occasional holding of hands a halfhearted gesture against this.

I'm trying hard to run some films of the past through my head, to see something that explains, shows the closeness and emotion there was between us, Mark. Some image that perfectly captures what I think I remember. But the moments of grace have not been fixed in solid matter. I'm no longer sure how much I've invented for my memories. The rings are small inside me.

Cards and Telegrams

Dear Mother and Dad,

Thanks for the birthday package for Sam. He loved everything. We're looking forward to seeing you all in August. Warm regards to Mark and his wife. Please excuse the postcard—it's all I had handy.

Love,
Arla

Joe. Received arrival date. See you September.

Arla

Poetry

Imagining the Death of My Parents

wild horses gallop when they're alive
but not when they're dead
except in the dreams of those who loved them
their sleek browns and blacks
making shady spots in the hot white

brains of the bereaved

their hooves pat patting on grey matter
over and over and over again
throat sounds way off in the distance
far from the image in the brain
their sounds in the horizon sky

a storm that has passed over

sometimes these runners have riders

(the headless horseman)

and sometimes they are riderless

sometimes they become the famous
image of one riderless horse galloping

wild horses may also stand still
in the green grass, their hooves
taking root and leaves
springing from their ears

Questions

Dear Sam, I'm sorry I don't have enough patience for the million questions you ask every day. Why do we live in a house? Why not in a car? Why do you have two arms? Why not three? How come Raggedy Ann has no bones and I do? Why do we sit on chairs? Why don't glasses have feet? Why aren't knees elbows? How come nighttime isn't daytime? How long is 10 minutes? But I should be grateful you're still asking about objects and quantities. Next year the questions may be harder.

I wonder what you will have to say to me in 20 years.

Questions for Sam:
What was it like in the womb?

How did it feel to be a baby, to suck milk from my breasts and not distinguish your body from mine? (That's what is said about infants. But maybe it's not true.)

What is the significance of the fact that you cannot remember these things at all? Are they part of some mystery we will never have access to?

Is memory different from dreams?

THE SAINT
w h o
FREQUENTED
PROSTITUTES

THE SAINT WAS SLIM, not very tall, and had a quiet, gentle charm about him. He had pale blue eyes and long, thin fingers. He looked, in short, as saints tend to look. Small children and animals preferred his company over that of other adults. His body moved through the air like the slender reeds of Chinese brush paintings.

His name was Francis, which made a lot of sense, and I picked him out of 100 responses to a companion ad I had placed in the paper. I was four years separated from my husband, and my small son needed someone to set an example of how to pee standing up. I was tired of wiping the tiles, and, to confess, I was lonely.

I didn't tell anyone I was putting an ad in the paper. While everyone I knew was saying how it was becoming a respectable practice, they always added, "but I would never do it." It was really still something that kinks or losers did, and none of us was a kink or loser.

I had endured five boring afternoon drinks before I met with Francis. He wasn't especially goodlooking, but he had that easy grace and air of kindness, and I was attracted to him. I liked his work—studying the effect of insecticides on food crops. This endeavour seemed, like him, quiet and graceful, and it had the advantage of being forward-thinking and moral. As work that was clearly and directly useful to humans, it was a nice complement to the murkier profession I had come to consider my own—artist. My four-year-old son Sam had been agitating for a man around the house. He had taken to handing me pictures torn from magazines like *Toronto Life* to give me an idea of the type he preferred, and had begun actively recruiting for me. I would take him to parties (to save the babysitting fee) and he'd ask the first man who pleased his fancy, "Would you come home with my mom?" So I knew he wouldn't mind if I started seeing someone on a regular basis.

In the social custom of our time, Francis and I went to bed right away and then proceeded to get to know each other.

But it wasn't that simple. The sex, in fact, never really got off the ground. Most people have a case of the nerves the first or second time and things get better later; some people only like it the first few times and then get a case of the nerves. Francis had a prolonged case of the nerves, from the beginning on through. But he would not admit to that. "Be patient. The passion will come," he said, and he told me stories about how women praised his slow and gentle way of making love. When I complained, he told me I was being male and goal-oriented, and this shut me up on the subject for months.

In the meantime, passion of the mental sort found its way into our lives through lengthy discussions in bed about our past. Francis had had several out-of-body experiences and had even made contact with previous incarnations of himself. He was dead serious about these stories and even made me promise not to tell other people, as he felt that he lost something of the experience for himself each time he told the stories. And there was nothing in it for him, he said, in trying to convince nonbelievers who found it all mildly amusing.

My friends wanted to know about Francis. "He is unusual," I said. "He's a receiver. I think he's a saint." They looked at me without comment, but I knew they thought my politics were deteriorating.

My son loved him. For hours, Francis played the sort of silly kids' games with Sam that most adults could stand for only a few minutes, and he had that undemanding charm and affection with my son that initially attracted me. When Francis said he wanted to live with me, I agreed. I told my son and he was ecstatic. It was winter; we decided to wait for the warm weather and get a place together.

Sam began making unfavourable comparisons between me and Francis: how come Francis never shouts and you do? How come Francis doesn't mind if I wake him up in the morning and you do? I quelled my desire to brag about my three years of diapering and getting up at all hours of the night and other stories of single-mother martyrdom and said something like, "Everybody is different." I was, however, pissed off at the saint.

I knew Francis had been separated from his wife and three children for a long time, perhaps ten years, because he had told me that right away. After a while I wanted to meet his kids. "They're teenagers," Francis said, "they're always busy. It's hard to get an appointment. I see them for dinner every few weeks."

After a few months I was invited to one of these dinners. Francis' two darkhaired daughters said hardly a word to me, glancing up occasionally from the spaghetti dinner Francis had cooked to stare at my hair, then my eyes, later my breasts, and, when I got up to get some water, my rear end and the width of my hips. If only I could have the grace with kids that Francis has, I thought, and put everyone at ease. Francis's blonde, fair-skinned son rattled on incessantly about his collection of model airplanes, while we nodded and said "uh-hunh" every so often. The daughters and the son were unlike in looks and manner, but they seemed close in spirit; beneath the hum of the son's monologue, a privileged three-way conversation of the eyes bound the siblings together and curtained them off from Francis and me.

When dinner was over, they got up immediately to leave, all three of them at once, like a small platoon, while Francis cleared the table. I felt responsible for the silence and said, "What's the rush? Stay a while and let's talk." All four of them turned and looked at me stiffly, Francis at the sink, and the kids in single file at the door, holding their jackets.

"Oh well," I said, "if you have to go, that's okay, we'll talk more the next time."

"Yeah, okay," said the son, sharing a dark glance with his dark sisters.

"We might go on a camping trip later in the summer. Maybe you'd all like to come," I said.

The son looked at Francis, immobile at the sink, hands mid-air, grasping sponge and dish. "Go on a trip with *him*?" the son asked, pausing, then opening his eyes wide, "and *you*?"

"Yeah, well, just a thought, anyway, maybe some other time. Nice to meet you all," I mumbled.

"Nice to meet you," they said, properly, and left.

Francis had resumed washing dishes and I went over to dry and put them away. "What was that all about?" I asked. Francis didn't answer. "What's the matter? Are you okay?" I asked again.

He didn't say "yes" or "no" or "leave me alone," just kept washing.

"Can't you say something?" I asked.

"I can't," he said, and he went upstairs and lay down on the bed.

The next night we got into bed and I braced myself for some non-goal-oriented foreplay, but instead of touching me, Francis lay on his back and said, "I want to tell you something."

"Okay," I said.

"I love you," he said. "I can feel it. You're in my heart. I want you to know my worst secrets."

My heart bulged painfully into my breastbone and I rubbed it with my left hand. "Go on," I said.

"When I left my wife and kids," he said, "I started seeing prostitutes. I had a good job and I could afford it. I did it for about a year." He stopped, apparently to give me an opportunity to digest his small bomb. He looked at me. I looked at him.

"Are you upset?" he asked.

"Yes" did not seem like the right thing to say. I breathed in, then out, then in again, to have something that my words could ride out on, to create a cushion of air for them to nestle into, be protected by.

"Well, I'm glad you told me," I said. "It's not exactly a story I'm glad is yours. I don't know. What can I say?"

We spent some more quiet moments looking at each other's faces, as though the eyes might take over where the mouths had failed.

"What was it like?" my mouth asked.

He laughed. Was he relieved at my reaction? He breathed in, and a whole attic of words came out with the exhalation. I could smell the dust and cobwebs.

"Well, I saw high-class prostitutes, call girls, you'd say, I guess. I had regulars. They really liked me. They said they wanted to see me on the side, as a friend, for free, but said they couldn't, that it would get them in trouble. There was one I used to call and she would say, 'I was thinking about you. I'm so glad you called.'"

Francis's speech gave me time to position myself safely—I imagined a football field of objectivity separating us, allowing me to see things scientifically. It could be a field of sociology, it could be psychology, I could just analyze the whole thing, and keep my heart and breastbone out of it.

"They just said that stuff to get your business," I blurted out. The football field fell into a black hole; Francis and I were up against each other raw.

"I don't think so," he said, insulted. "You're saying that because you're upset. Just think of some of the creeps they must have seen. I think they liked me. It was a relief to spend time with me instead of a weirdo."

"Maybe," I said.

"But you are upset, aren't you?" he asked again.

"I don't know. It was a long time ago," I said, "it was after your marriage broke up. I don't know, I suppose a lot of men do that, and don't tell anyone. Why did you do it?"

"It was easy," he said. "I mean the sex was easy. It wasn't with my wife. Easy, that is. After she had a baby I just couldn't get into it. But it was easy with the prostitutes. I paid my money and got exactly what I wanted."

"And didn't have to give anything in return," I said.

Francis didn't reply. His lips tightened and his nostrils flared.

"Sorry, I didn't mean to shut you up," I said. Objectivity, I thought. Get into the issue. "What kind of girls did you like?"

"When I was paying? When I'm paying, I like blond. And fair skin." My hand jerked up to my brown hair. My ears took note of the shift in tenses. Francis didn't notice my gesture; he was looking off into the distance, watching a film unroll.

"What did you do? Did you kiss?"

"Look, that's enough. I don't want to talk about this right now."

"I thought you did want to talk about it."

"I don't like being interrogated."

We were both lying on our backs looking at the ceiling. I turned onto my side, facing him, and touched his shoulder. He lay still for a minute, then turned his back to me and fell asleep immediately.

I stayed up and read magazines for a long time. I woke before him in the morning and lay still, waiting for him to wake up. When he began to stir, I touched his back and said, "Thanks for telling me what you told me last night. I respect you for that."

"I'm glad I told you," he said. "Do you love me?"

"Yes, I think so. I want to love you."

I WANTED TO TALK ABOUT the prostitutes again, but Francis didn't. I also wanted to talk about our sex life, but Francis didn't. He said, "I love you. The passion will come. I can feel it." And then he would go silent. If I persisted, he would go to sleep.

I was glad I had found a man who was ready to play father to my son. I was glad I wasn't going to be lonely, but I was not glad about sex. I felt guilty for thinking it so important, and I felt politically amiss for being goal-oriented, but I still felt dissatisfied and it got worse. The sessions of prolonged foreplay became less frequent, and the sleeping and silence more frequent. Something nagged at me about the prostitute story, our sex life, and Francis's alternating speeches and silences. The feeling took root in me that there was more, a lot more, which he had not told me.

One night I was alone at my house and Francis was

at his apartment, and I could no longer control the feeling that there was something I didn't know about Francis that I needed to know, something we needed to talk about that he was refusing me. The feeling beat about my inner organs like a trapped butterfly, no, a bat, trying to get out.

I phoned him. "You are lying to me," I said the instant he picked up the phone. I didn't even say "hello." "I don't know what you are lying about, but you are lying to me. You're a liar." I was shouting. And a little worried. What if he wasn't a liar? What if I was crazy? But the bat wanted out.

Francis never shouted. He said quietly, "You're upset. Go to sleep. We'll talk later."

I hung up the phone and unplugged the jack. When I woke up at seven a.m., I plugged the jack in and it rang immediately. Francis's voice was hoarse and ragged, unrested. It said, "You're right. I'm lying. I've been lying for six months, since I've known you. I'm still seeing prostitutes. I've been seeing them for 10 years, and I've been seeing them all the time I've been seeing you. I saw one the afternoon after I met you. I saw one the day after I told you I loved you. I don't know why. I wish I knew why. Something comes over me and I can't help myself. I'm sorry," he said, and began to cry over the phone. "Can I come over later and talk to you?"

"All right," I said. I felt burning and cold at the same time, like hot ice. I hung up the phone and punched the table.

It's one thing to catch your husband developing this habit after 10 years of marriage. It's another for a guy supposed to be in the first bloom of love. Not to mention he was shooting the juices I wanted into someone else. Goal-oriented, my ass. *He* was goal-oriented. I just happened to be part of his warm-up procedure, not part of the endgame. And my kid, for christ's sake. What was I supposed to do now? Somewhere inside me a little voice said I should feel sorry for Francis, who had cried on the phone, but I was hurt, betrayed, and furious, and I told the voice to fuck off. It was probably Francis's voice anyway. He was having an out-of-body experience in my body.

He arrived after lunch with flowers and chocolate eclairs. We stood still in the kitchen staring at each other for a minute. Francis had tears in his eyes. I took the paper bag with the eclairs in it and stepped on it. I took the flowers and tore them up and threw them around the room.

My son appeared at that moment. "Hi, Francis," he shouted, and ran up and hugged him. Francis knelt down and put his arms around Sam, looking up sorrowfully at me, like he was my victim, looking back at Sam, back at me again, eyes pleading and pitiful.

"Oh shit," I said. "Look, Sam, you get out of here. Go up and watch TV. Leave us alone," I said, beginning to raise my voice.

Francis said quietly, "Your mom's upset. You go up and I'll see you later."

Sam looked angrily at me, gave Francis a kiss, and left.

Francis fell into a silence, not the withdrawn, unfriendly silence he used to take on when he wanted to put an end to a conversation, especially to my questions, but a helpless silence. His eyes stared out the kitchen window, looking, perhaps, for a third party to intervene. I stood like a petrified tree stump, immobile with fury.

After long minutes, he turned his face to me, his saintly composure scuttled. "Please come see my therapist, please talk to her. Please," he said. His voice whimpered and his eyes were wet.

My ability to analyze was shot to hell, and my heart was beating on different drums in all four corners of the kitchen. I didn't know what I thought, or what I felt. The signals were loud, but incomprehensible.

"That sounds like a terrible idea," I said. "Okay. I'll do it."

I PHONED FRANCIS'S THERAPIST that afternoon. "Oh yes," said the receptionist when I said my name, "she'll see you first thing tomorrow morning. Nine a.m. She charges $70 an hour."

"Okay," I said.

I arrived the next morning and was not kept waiting. The secretary announced me cheerfully over an office intercom, and a middle-aged woman with long brown hair, black eye make-up, and a save-the-whales button emerged, smiling. She ushered me into a white office with white canvas chairs, and overstuffed white pillows on the floor. Her hand on my arm was gentle. Too gentle, I thought.

"How are you feeling?" she asked me, her voice full of compassion as I declined a floor pillow and lowered myself into a canvas chair, sitting up straight, and placing my arms on the white wooden arms of the chair.

"Anxious," I said. "Anxious as hell. Depressed. Worthless." I had a good cry, finally.

She handed me a box of tissues and let me cry. When I stopped, she said, "I understand how you feel. You've been through a lot."

"Francis is a mirage," I said.

"I don't think Francis is a mirage," she countered, calmly, conversationally, smiling. "Well, that hasn't been my experience."

I tightened my grip on the box of tissues she had given me.

"He is *too*," I said. I wanted to start screaming, "He is too, he is too, he is too," and throw things. But I said quietly, again, "He's a mirage."

"I've had a different experience with Francis..." she hesitated, deciding whether to continue in this vein, and changed her mind. "You know, it's a turning point in his therapy that he told you about all this. You've been a catalyst in some way. I'm really pleased." She kept her voice pleasant, but from within her eyes something glared at me, angry. She wants something from me, and I'm not cooperating. I'm fucking up her script.

I took a tissue from the box still in my possession and wiped my eyes. "Glad to be useful," I said. "I think he's a fucking mirage. I think he's a fake."

What was I doing here? Why had I come? Is this a consultation on Francis? She sure isn't treating me like a client, but then why had the secretary told me the cost of the session?

"I've had a different experience with Francis." She was back there again. "Do you know his children?" she asked, ever friendly.

"Yeah," I said. "Do you?"

She frowned. Shrinks don't like being asked questions, I remembered.

"Yes, I do," she answered reluctantly. I could see her telling herself it was okay to yield a small part of control of the situation to me. She was going to allow me some questions, and she was going to respond. "They have an affectionate communication. I find that moving. Don't you?"

"How long has he been in therapy with you, anyway?" I was going to hang on to my position as questioner.

"Two years," she said.

"Maybe you don't know Francis so well yourself. Did you know about this prostitute stuff?" I asked her.

"Not that he was doing it while he was seeing you. Only that he used to. But I think it's great he told you, and me. It's a breakthrough for him. A lot of men do the same thing and never tell anyone."

"I made him tell me. He wouldn't have told me if I hadn't made him."

"I can see that that's how you feel about it."

"What else have you two been talking about lately?" I asked.

She weighed this inquiry in her mind and decided it was time to take up the slack in the short leash she'd let me out on.

"I can't break a client's confidentiality," she said, with smooth sympathy, "but I do know that he cares about you." She paused for a moment to consider what she should say. "He does tell me about some of the times he's enjoyed with you, like that dinner you both had with his kids."

"Oh," I said, "that's interesting." And I closed my mouth ostentatiously. I stared silently at the whale on her button. If I couldn't ply her with questions, I'd fight her with silence. She allowed this to continue a minute or so.

"What are you thinking about now?" she asked, foolishly handing me the advantage.

"The time," I said flatly. She straightened her back

and raised her eyelids a little. I relented. "I'm sorry, but I do have to leave. I have another appointment. Thanks for your time. I appreciate it. I really do." I smiled.

"That's okay," she said. "I'm glad I could help. Francis has come a long way, and I know he's going to make it. We can either help or hurt the situation. I'm sure you'd like things to be better, wouldn't you?"

"Yes, sure, better. But it seems really hard," I said.

"I hear you saying you want to try. Can you say that? Try it. Say you want to try."

Is she really saying that to me? Leave it to Francis to have a shrink who talks to her clients like they were children.

"I can't say that right now."

"Just try. I think you can." And she placed her hand over mine, the one holding the tissue box. We stared at each other, wall against wall, the box our only point of connection.

"Listen," I said, "I'll come back another time and try to say I want to try. I don't want to say it today." I folded my arms and crossed my legs. Her hand slid off mine, and the tissue box fell to the floor. So there. I almost stuck my tongue out.

"I can see that's how you feel," she said flatly, picking up the tissue box and placing it on the table next to her. The feeling behind her eyes was slipping into her voice.

"Look, you've been working on him for two years. How about giving me two days, okay?" I looked at the tissues, which were out of reach. I'd have to get all the way out of the chair and take a step to get them. The hell with them, anyway. I'll be damned if I'm going to cry for this woman again. She can have the tissues.

"Call me next week, and we'll make an appointment," she said, her voice even, her lips tight.

"Okay," I said, picking up my bag and rising from the chair.

"Since it's been half a session, you only have to pay me $35," she said.

"I think you'd better put that on Francis's bill," I said.

"Well, I don't know. I didn't discuss that with him."

"Believe me, it's okay," I said. "He asked me to come here. It was his idea. Anyway, I don't have any money with me and I left my chequebook home, so you'll have to do it that way."

"I'll bill you," she said.

"You do that."

"Well, good luck. It's hard to be a single mother. I really admire women like you."

"Thanks, I'll call you," I said, as neutrally as I could muster.

I walked home with the little voice asking me to be compassionate. "Fuck you," I said to it, and picked up speed.

Before I called Francis to tell him it was over I had to talk to Sam. I would have preferred another chat with Francis's shrink to the session with my kid.

"I'm not going to see Francis any more."

"Oh, Mom, you promised. You said we were all going to live together. Oh, Mom," Sam said, and started to cry.

"Would you like to know why?" I asked.

"No," he said, crying.

"Well, I'm going to tell you anyway. It's because he lied to me for a long time about something important. It's because he doesn't love me. It's because I need something more. I'll find someone else."

"I want to talk to Francis. What's his side of the story?" Sam said, still crying.

"I'm telling the truth," I said.

"I know," he said. "I just want to hear the other story."

Four years old and he wants to hear the other side of the story. I wished I would cry and maybe he would give me a break. But I couldn't. All I could feel was that icy cold inside, and my forehead hot. "I can't let you talk to him. It's about stuff you wouldn't understand."

"I could understand. I understand lots of stuff," he said.

"I don't think you'd understand this. I'm sorry. Be patient. There'll be someone else."

"I don't want anyone else. I want *Francis*. I *love* Francis. I want to talk to Francis," he sobbed.

"I'll think it over," I said, not knowing what else to say. I thought about Francis and his children and doubted he'd want to see Sam anyway, if I...if I abandoned him.

That's the way Francis would look at it. That I'd abandoned him. Whichever way I turned, that's how it was going to look. I hugged Sam.

He pulled away and stopped crying. "I'm going to play upstairs," he said.

"Hey, Sam," a kid's voice from the backyard called through the kitchen window. "Wanna play?"

Sam went to the window. "Hi, Tommy, yeah," he said, "let's play in my room. Let's play Lego."

"Okay," said Tommy.

Sam let him in and they headed upstairs.

"Does your mom love you?" I heard Sam ask Tommy.

"Yeah, sure. Does your mom love you?"

"Yeah, I guess so," said Sam. "Do you think your mom would ever leave you?"

"No."

"How come?"

"It's against the law."

"Oh, no kidding. Oh," said Sam, his voice full of relief.

"Yeah," said Tommy.

I reached for the phone to dial Francis's number. As his phone began to ring, a scratchy noise, like a clearing of the throat, began in my brain. "Fuck you," I said to the little voice, before it could even start arguing with me.

PRETTY GOLDFISH

DURING BRAN FLAKES SAM notices that Pretty Goldfish is belly up. "What's the fish doing, Arla?" he asks.

"I'd rather be called Mom," I say. "Why do you keep calling me Arla?"

"Because that's your name," Sam says. "Don't be dumb."

"Maybe you could try 'Mom' once in a while."

"Everybody's called Mom. Nobody's called Arla. It's special."

"But Mom makes me feel like I'm special to you," I say.

Sam sighs. "Okay, I'll try and do it sometimes. What about the *fish*, Arla. What's the matter with the fish?"

I look at the goldfish bowl. "Oh no. It's dead."

"What do you mean, *he's dead*? How come? How come he's dead? Is he really dead? How come?"

After a minute, I say, "I think it was just time for it to die, you know. Fish don't live a really long time. I think it just died because it had lived as long as it was supposed to."

Sam's eyes get red and wet. He's going to cry. Okay, I say to myself, say the right thing. Remember what they said in the effective parenting workshop. Validate feelings. I'm supposed to validate how he's feeling, that's right. Don't say it's nothing, that it's the fish's time to go, say he is right to feel whatever he feels. Right.

"I know you feel sad," I say. "You liked Pretty Goldfish a lot. You can cry if you want, it's okay, you know."

Sam immediately dries his eyes with a napkin and gets himself under control. "You don't care that he's dead. It's not fair," he says, angry. "It's too short. It's not like people. People have a long time. It's not fair for Pretty Goldfish."

I panic and regress to pre-workshop thinking. "It seems longer to a fish than it does to you," I say. "For the fish it feels as long as a person's life feels to a person." It seems like a good thing to say in the circumstances.

Pretty lived for six months, in fact, which is longer than I expected. We bought it one day in Woolworth's, after me and Sam and Norman had all jammed into a twenty-five-cent photo machine booth and made fools of ourselves in front of crowds of Saturday shoppers. When we came out of the booth we found ourselves face to face with a huge tank filled with hundreds of goldfish.

"Let's get a fish!" Sam screamed.

"Yeah, all right!" Norman and I shouted back at him.

"Your first pet!" Sam had just turned five.

It took Sam 20 minutes to study all the fish. To me, each one was a perfect gold twin of the last, but Sam could grasp their individual essence.

Finally, he pointed to one toward the bottom of the tank, swimming away from the pack. "That one," he said. "That's a pretty one."

It was with relief that I watched Sam take a mothering attitude toward the fish. I figured that meant I was nice to Sam, even if I hadn't studied effective parenting until he was five, and that the reason Sam was turning out so good had something to do with my mothering. Maybe, on the other hand, I told myself, Sam had a wonderful nature that no amount of fucked-up parenting could destroy.

Pretty lived on the big wooden kitchen table where we took all our meals. We'd bought one of those ordinary small goldfish bowls and the fish twitched and darted around and was always hungry. You're supposed to feed fish once a day or they get overfed and die, Norman said, but it became obvious that Pretty, like the rest of us, took three regular meals. If it hadn't been fed, it would slam itself against the sides of the fishbowl as it swam and jerked back and forth. When I picked up the red fishfood can and approached the bowl, it stopped dead, then swam straight up to the surface, nose first, as though suddenly pulled there by a heavenly fishing pole.

Looking back on it, I think I was a little insensitive to Pretty. I didn't buy any greens or plants or other things that fish like. The fish looked lonely in the barren bowl one morning, so I took a green marble frog from the mantelpiece and plunked it in. I guess I expected Pretty to swim over and give it a pucker, but instead the fish seized up, darted to the other side of the bowl, and stayed there, dead still, for an hour. Finally, it slowly approached the frog and nosed around it, then began swimming about as usual. I felt better about nearly scaring the fish to death when, later, Pretty began to use the frog to hide behind when it felt anti-social.

Pretty quadrupled in size in about a month and, at its death, was at least ten times bigger than when we had bought it. If we had put it in the bathtub, it probably would have become as big as a cat. We fed it well, but it was still nervous, even when it wasn't hungry. I took this as a reflection on me, of course. But then, I asked myself, how come I don't have a nervous kid? It was nature-nurture again. The old question.

Maybe it was Norman's effect on the fish. Norman and I had lived together for six months, and he was playing stepdad to Sam. Norman was nice but had high anxiety about his health and his conversations with other grown-ups. He was great with Sam and had almost gotten used to me, though talking with me still made him nervous sometimes. He also had a touch of the passive-aggressive in him, never being one to raise his voice, but preferring to lie down in bed with the covers over his head in the middle of an argument. He was a tall, thin man who ate tons of food but, unlike Pretty Goldfish, never gained weight. But if Norman had made the fish nervous, how come he hadn't made Sam nervous? To tell the truth, I have not been a calm individual myself, but rather the high-strung, explosive, heart attack type, averaging one burst of temper a week. These often took place in the kitchen where there were more breakable things to choose from. Since the fish bowl was in the kitchen, you could have pinned Pretty's nervousness on me. Then again, I had not managed in five years to stress my son, or at least he didn't show it. So it was either that nothing could make Sam nervous because he was such a remarkable, centred child (*my* remarkable, centred child) or that nothing could make the fish calm because it had such a fragile, nervous nature to begin with.

Sam became attached to the fish, of course. More than that, he granted it a natural and rightful place in the house in a way that never occurred to me or Norman. We were playing a number game at dinner and Sam gave us a question: Who's the youngest member of the family?

We guessed him, then each other, each time Sam saying "no" with a big smile. We gave up and Sam shouted, "It's the *fish*,! Ha, ha, you lose!"

"How do you know Pretty Goldfish felt that way?" Sam says, his wet eyes staring at the upside-down fish. "How do you know he felt his life was long? Maybe he felt short."

"I read it in a book," I say, feeling guilty.

"I want another pet," Sam says. "I want a pet that doesn't die fast. How about a cat? Does a cat die fast?"

"No, a cat lives about 15 years," I say.

"Okay, let's get a cat."

This seems a disrespectful conversation over the freshly dead body of Pretty Goldfish, but Sam had a deeper emotional relationship with the fish than me, to say the least, and I'm not about to criticize him. "Let's talk it over with Norman," I say. "Cats are more work than fish, and cost more money, and are more trouble. We'll have to think it over."

"Okay, we'll talk with Norman tonight," Sam says.

Norman has a meeting at work and doesn't get home till Sam is asleep. I can't give him the bad news straight. "Guess what?" I say, after he's taken his coat and shoes off and collapsed on the sofa.

"Animal, vegetable or mineral?" he asks.

"Animal," I say.

He sits up. "You're pregnant," he says, his face grey.

"Nope, try again."

"Okay, you said it's animal, right?"

"Right."

"Animal–human or animal–animal?"

"Animal–animal."

"The fish died."

"Right."

Norman looks genuinely sad. I tell him how it went with Sam. "Maybe we should talk to him some more about it," I say. "Death has been a big topic of conversation this year. And now we have our first practical example. Show and tell. The only thing is, I don't really know what to say."

"Just don't give him that 'everything dies' stuff. I don't think he's conscious of his own death yet. He's only five."

"Oh yes, he is, he's conscious of it, there were some conversations that went on around here before you came on board," I say ungenerously. "What's wrong with saying, 'everything dies.' It does. Dying is part of living, you know." I wince at my cozy motto.

"I don't think putting it like that does much good," Norman says. "I think we should just tell him it's okay to be sad, that we're sad, too, and that we all miss Pretty Goldfish." Norman has also attended the effective parenting workshop.

"He wants a cat."

"Well, maybe we'll get a cat."

"What should we do about the fish?"

"I guess the three of us could bury it in the backyard tomorrow."

"Can we leave it overnight in the bowl, or is it going to rot and stink up the kitchen?" I ask.

"Oh, I don't think fish rot so fast when they're in water. Besides, it's so small. How much of a stink could it make? We can wait till tomorrow," Norman says.

We go into the kitchen to get ourselves a drink, and it has already begun to smell from Pretty Goldfish. "Looks like we have to do something tonight. I'll empty the bowl and put some ice in it and put the fish back in," I say. Norman scoops the fish out of the bowl with a soup spoon and puts it on a dish.

The bright gold colour has already faded to a pale yellow. The belly is white and a greyish translucent jelly coats the perfectly round eyes, white with solid black centres. Where the belly has begun to rot, in the centre, it is pinkish brown. The tiny-scaled skin looks slimy and sticky. The fish lies completely still on the dish, like a sardine, like any dead fish, its nervous spirit gone and departed.

Norman grimaces. "You wouldn't think such a small fish would smell so much," he says.

He washes out the bowl and I fill it with two trays of ice cubes, scoop Pretty up again and put it on the ice. Its nose slides down between two cubes. "This is really stupid," I say. "Why don't I just wrap it up and put it in the freezer. This ice is going to melt, by morning the water will be warm and smelly. Putting it in the freezer is easier, anyway."

"Just wrap it in tin foil and put it in the fridge, that's the best thing to do. Then we can bury it inside the tin foil," says Norman.

"Can't we just bury it as is? Do we really need a coffin?" I say.

Norman's face shows suffering. "Arla, how are you going to carry it out to the garden—by its smelly tail?"

"Yeah, okay, you're right." I get the tin foil and try to get the fish out of the ice cubes. This is hard, because it keeps slipping between them. I'm afraid if I spill the whole thing out, the cubes will fall on the fish and break it to pieces. But I can't get it out and finally I tip everything into a large dish. The fish emerges in one piece. I touch its side with my forefinger, and it feels surprisingly solid. I suddenly get a catch in my throat.

"This is ridiculous," I say to Norman. "I'm getting upset."

"I know," he says, "I'm upset too."

"God knows I've seen a lot of dead fish."

"You know," Norman confesses, "I saw the fish up near the top of the water last night and it looked like it was gasping a bit for air and I told myself maybe I should change the water and then I was tired and decided to do it the next day."

"Oh, for christ's sake, don't start guilting yourself about the fish," I say. "We didn't expect it to last a month. I thought you said six months was a long life for a fish."

"I don't know," Norman says. "I don't know how long fish are supposed to live. My brother kept fish and they died every month. He kept buying more. He loved fish."

I get some tin foil, nudge the fish onto it with my finger, wrap it up and put it in the freezer.

In the morning when we get up, we find Sam pretend-reading to his stuffed bears. I'm in the washroom when I hear Sam say, "Norman, I've got some bad news for you."

"What's that?" Norman asks.

"The fish died."

Norman has forgotten all about it. So have I.

"I know," Norman says. I can feel him gathering up his internal resources as he next says, "Let's sit down and talk about it."

"Wait for me!" I shout from the washroom. "I'm coming, too." I rush down the hallway and Norman is sitting on the bed with Sam on his lap, asking him how he feels about the fish dying.

"Sad," Sam says. "I want a cat."

"It's okay to be sad," Norman and I say simultaneously. Sam stares at both of us.

"It's not okay. It's bad," Sam says.

"I'm sad, too," I say.

"Me, too," says Norman.

"The fish's spirit is still alive," I say.

Sam looks at me and says, "*Arla.*"

"Do you want to talk some more about it?" Norman asks.

"I want to get up," Sam says. He gets off Norman's lap and goes to play with his bears.

"We'll talk with him some more later," Norman says to me, and gets his coat to go to work.

He goes to Sam's room to say goodbye. "I'll see you later," he says. "I'll see you tonight."

"I'll see you tonight," Sam says, cheerfully. "And tomorrow, too. And the next day. I'll see you forever."

Norman goes down the stairs.

"I'll see you till you're dead," Sam calls after him.

FOREPLAY *to* LOVE

ONE CHRISTMAS, WHEN SAM was in Australia visiting Joe, I was given an electrical massager with eight attachments. It came in a bright red box with a shiny silver cover. *Foreplay to Love* was printed in gold script and under it was a picture of a naked man and woman in gentle embrace. It was to afford me with a moment of grace, one of those epiphanies you can count on the fingers of one hand every few decades, if you're lucky. And I'm nothing if not lucky. At the time, for example, I was having a passionate romance.

Terry was very handsome, very tall, very broadshouldered, and an accomplished lover. He was large, goodlooking, and powerful—like the Chrysler Building. In fact, when he told me he loved me I felt that a building had fallen on me. There was no alternative but to be in love back.

"Well, I'm in love with you," he said, scratching his head in the middle of a conversation about how to clean fish. "I don't know why. You're not beautiful."

It's hard to speak when you're under a building, and I didn't say anything.

Terry said, "I have to go to the washroom."

He left the bedroom; I peeked out the doorway and watched him from behind as he steered his big, naked beautiful body down the hallway to the bathroom. I shook my head in wonder at what had arrived in my apartment, declaring its love. Making his way through the corridor, Terry looked like an upside-down boat, his wide stern of shoulders nearly grazing the walls of the apartment canal as his walking swayed him from side to side, the prow of his feet bravely carrying the towering mass forward. Fortunately, nothing was in the way.

I waited for the inner glow of being loved to spread outward through my body from my heart. Instead, a grey shadow descended on me from the place Terry had been sitting on the bed, settling like a dirty sheet over my body, entangling my limbs. I couldn't move, and breathing was no easy matter either. Terry returned. His grey ghost lifted and rejoined his body; I was able to speak.

"I guess I love you, too," I said. He accepted that as natural and made love to me.

The trouble with being big, tall, and good-looking

is that everyone expects everything else about you to be perfect. This is the root of the oppression of the beautiful people. Terry was not perfect. He was clever and had a big mouth, but he was short-tempered, egocentric, rude, illogical, and disorganized. He was irresponsible and incapable of linear thinking. In short, he could not hold a job. I drifted into propping Terry up, mending fences with people he had insulted, and making sure I had money so he wouldn't starve—even though he had never starved before he'd met me—but then again, others had been doing this job.

I knew that Terry needed to maintain an image of perfection, and that it was up to me to help him do this.

Both my family and his lived in New York and we went to visit them during Christmas week. Terry had presented me with the electric massager before we left. We used it once after making love, and I came so sharp and strong that I drew my legs together violently and doubled up. I thought I was going to pee all over Terry. It was that kind of orgasm.

I was going to release everything.

We took the massager with us on our trip. The proximity of family bedrooms was nerve-wracking and the machine stayed in its box, lying cold, white and plastic under the shiny silver cover.

My father suffered from chronic undiagnosed heart pains and my mother from severe colds and periodic depression. But they were enjoying a rare spell of good health, both of them at the same time. This, said my brother, was because it had been such a long time since my last visit. I would have stopped speaking to him for a year over this remark, but his wife was eight months pregnant and, to be generous at such a time, I dismissed it as run-of-the-mill sibling rivalry. It was an unusually happy period for my relatives. A new baby was on its way and my parents were feeling well.

I have a lot of relatives and at any given time some of them are not speaking to others. This is the case now and it was the case then. So instead of having one big family bash, we succumbed to pressure from my mother and drove all over the five boroughs of New York City, visiting Aunt Bertha, Aunt Rose and Uncle Max, Cousin Leonard, the two Miltons, and so on, one visit at a time.

We also spent five days at my parents' house, one at my brother's, two with Terry's undemanding *goyisha* family, and two in New York City getting culture. These last four days created a situation of stress for my mother. "You come to New York once in a blue moon and all you do is run around," she said. I replied that we had spent most of the time with her and her relatives and even drew up a calendar chart as an accompanying graphic, but she remained unconvinced. The day before we left she came down with a cold. On the day we left she went to the doctor and was diagnosed as having bronchitis. When we said goodbye to my father, he put his right hand on his chest, apologized for not being able to get up, and wished us a good trip.

We packed our bags and wrapped the massager in a pair of blue jeans and placed it on the bottom of the suitcase under Terry's shirts where it wouldn't be seen by airport security inspectors. The visit had made us testy and we snapped and squinted at each other all the way home.

We got back on New Year's Day, traditional time of anti-social feelings and distaste for new beginnings. Terry and I both declared a need to be alone and went off to our own apartments.

The first thing I did when I got home was to take a nap and dream that Terry was standing outside my window. Terry, as I said, is tall and broad, but in the dream he was of medium height and thin, with narrow shoulders. He stood outside my open window carrying a basket of oranges (Terry loves oranges). His lips and forehead were damp. I lay naked on my bed looking at him. He put the oranges down and stepped through the open window and entered my body at the vagina, with his head—arms and hands flat at his sides—slithering through me like a snake, coming out my mouth face first, his toes scraping my ankles. He got stuck like that, his body inside mine, his face jutting in front of my face, his neck filling my throat, feet twisted around my knees, his legs clinging to mine. I stood up and tried to walk. With great difficulty I paced up and down my bedroom with Terry inside me. His feet uncurled from my knees and scraped along the floor.

The telephone woke me up. It was my brother calling to say that my mother was in the hospital with mild pneumonia, and that my father was having angina pains again and was also in hospital. The same one, in fact. Not only that, but my brother's wife, eight-and-a-half months pregnant, had been rushed to that very same hospital when her water broke. She was in labour and he had been holding her hand and breathing with her, until he had suddenly felt faint and gone into the corridor to get some air. I guess it seemed like the perfect time to call and get a few things off his chest. My brother was good at carrying forward family traditions, like the one of sharing the pain.

"Whatever you do, don't come and visit and make everything worse," he said. I assured him I wouldn't, wished him and his wife well, hung up the phone, lay down in bed, and pulled the quilt up over my head, leaving a tiny space for one eye to peek out.

I had dumped the contents of the suitcase on the bed and the massager and all its attachments were eyeball-to-eyeball in front of me. I plugged it in and, feeling reckless, turned it to top speed, something Terry and I had never done. Waves of heat and motion welled up and I felt that strong coming sensation. I breathed and relaxed and came. Suddenly arrows of heat shot from my belly down through my thighs and up again and I came once more, blackly, convulsively. I was in the lukewarm ocean bathtub of the world. I was in the universal womb. I was free.

I had wet my bed. I jumped up, ripped off the sheets before someone could come in and arrest me, and ran to the bathroom to wash myself with warm water. Then I sat down on the toilet and finished peeing. I felt great. The phone rang. It was my brother telling me his wife had just had a baby.

My relationship with Terry was never quite the same again and a few weeks later I broke up with him. I threw out the electric massager, which had served its purpose. I didn't think the experience could be duplicated and I wasn't sure I would survive a rerun. I never told Terry about my dream or my epiphany. In fact I never told anyone about it. But today is New Year's Day, the anniversary of a moment of grace, and it seems appropriate to write about it.

DONNA (and CARMINA)

DONNA HAD ONE OF THOSE FACES that is sometimes beautiful and sometimes ordinary. At times a clear-eyed, high-cheekboned, serene Mona Lisa, gazing at me with large and steady dark brown eyes. Holding my eyes gently in hers. Then she would have to scratch her arm. As she turned her face to watch her left hand reach over to her right forearm, strands of black hair would fall onto her forehead, and she looked suddenly messy, commonplace, short and frumpy, anybody in a crowd.

Donna was one of my students in a shortlived job I had teaching drawing at night to adult women at a community college. I was taken with her, attracted to her, gradually mesmerized, and finally disillusioned. With myself.

IT HAD BEEN QUITE A WHILE since taking up with a woman had caught my fancy. Carmina had been the last one. She'd attended a women's drawing class of my own invention, conducted in my living room, and advertised in handmade flyers I'd taped to telephone poles and bookstore bulletin boards. I'd started out with a dozen students, wound up with a loyal core group of half that. They still meet, today, without me. It's got to be one of the few halfway decent things I've done in my life, introducing those people to each other.

Carmina showed up at the first class before everyone else. "I have long admired you and your work," she said in a Spanish accent and husky voice. The accent was real, but I was dubious about the husk. I wondered how the admiration came about, since "my work" had appeared only a few times in hole-in-the-wall fringe galleries. Who cared?

I asked her what she knew about "my work," and she talked about the shows it had been in, describing my individual pieces. She'd been paying careful attention, that was clear.

"I went to the parties when the shows opened and I watched you talking with other people and I thought you were beautiful, but I was too shy to say hello. I have always been drawn to Jewish women, strongminded, with so much to say. *Feisty*, is that the word?" She pronounced it *fisty*. "I like that. And exotic. There's something so exotic and sensual about Jewish women, don't you think?"

It didn't sound like a shy speech to me. I was relieved to be stereotyped, as I felt myself doing the same thing to her, with her Spanish accent and husky voice. Anyway, feisty and sensual were okay. After all, she could have said pushy and sweaty.

"Then I saw your flyer at the Women's Bookstore and said to myself, enough, I am going to meet her. And here I am."

Here she was. A very beautiful woman with black hair and black eyes, full lips, smooth and clear honey-coloured skin, and a graceful, sexy, feminine body. Her face was always beautiful. It didn't matter which way Carmina turned, if her hair fell in her eyes, or if she scratched. She was stunning.

Carmina drew badly. One day she confessed to me that she really wanted to be a dancer, not an artist. She had enrolled in lessons and planned to really make a go at dancing.

"You *are* pushing 40," I said gently. "Do you think starting a dance career now is a good idea?"

"Well," she said, exuberantly, "perhaps instead I shall try...*acting!*" And she spread her arms wide, took a step forward and made a theatrical bow.

At every class, she arrived early and left late, hovering about me, talking and gazing, with no one else around.

I let it go on. One day she invited me to her apartment, "for tea, next Sunday."

What the hell, I thought. "Sure," I said.

There had been many times when I'd wondered if my life might not be more pleasant as a lesbian. I enjoyed men sexually but, all things being equal, preferred the friendship of women. On the whole, they were more intelligent, communicative, kinder, and I was easier with them. Despite a reasonable marriage of ten years' duration in my past, I had not otherwise had a sparkling history with men. And the designation "reasonable," for my marriage, was arrived at comparatively, based on the marriages I'd seen around me, none of which sparkled much. Unfortunately, men continued to be sexy for me more often than women.

In my twenties, when I was greedy for experience and anxious to check off a list of things I'd sampled in the world, I did some experimenting. First there was Margaret, really just an acquaintance, an activist in the same new-left organization I inhabited. She was only 17, skinny, flatchested, pale white, very WASP, and a self-declared dyke. *It's a passing phase which she'll outgrow* went the gossip. Why look a gift horse in the mouth? I said to myself. If I want to try that out, why not with someone who claimed to know what she was doing, who could show me how to make love with girls. Lesbianism 101: I decided to enroll.

I declared my interest to Margaret and she took me to bed. Or, rather, to couch. We stretched out on someone's sofa one night, while a party stormed elsewhere in an apartment, and felt each other's breasts and vaginas. She was easily as clumsy as me. I moved woodenly through the staged event, not enjoying getting my fingers sticky and wondering if I were sexually repressed. Margaret did not seem impassioned either.

So, my first sex experience with my own kind was a dud. It was clinical, allowing me to check off "have lesbian sexual experience" from my list of things to do, but not much else.

More interesting was my evening, later, with my dear friend Esther. We started out sitting naked in mixed company, about five of us checking off "have kinky group sex experience" from our lists of life experiences we wanted to be over with. Sensing my discomfort, Esther put her arm around me and smoothed my hair with her hand. She rubbed my shoulders and, somehow or other, as time went on, began to stroke my breasts, as everyone watched. She kissed me on the lips and I kissed her back. We looked coldly at the others and they left the room. Esther and I cuddled some more, feeling each other's bodies, hugging and kissing. It was like taking my favourite teddy bear to bed, but it did not feel sexy. We never got off, and we never had the urge to do it again.

Now here was this beautiful, accomplished, sexy

woman inviting me over. I'm being given another chance, I thought. If I can't get inspired with *her*, I really am a hopeless case.

I arrived at Carmina's apartment as the sun was going down on a winter Sunday. I had imagined "graciously appointed" decor with wild and flamboyant touches.

There was not a single piece of furniture in the living room, only a thick and soft grey carpet. Circling the entire room at the wooden molding between carpet and floor was one continuous, orange-plush pillow—a long, tubular, luxurious, comforting snake. Carmina offered me a corner and I sat down, cross-legged, resting my back against the orange snake, as the dark-orange light of sunset warmed the room.

"I have prepared some things to eat," she said, husky.

She went off to the kitchen and returned with a large tray of glossy-magazine gourmet treats: good cheeses on small rye bread, oysters and shrimp, caviar, melon and prosciutto, strawberries and chocolate, and, of course, wine. Candles and a crystal vase with three dark-red roses graced the tray. My throat contracted. Carmina placed the tray on the floor in front of me, lit the candles, stroked my hair, and said softly, "Eat."

"Aren't you going to join me?"

"No," she said. "I want to serve you."

She stood up and, as I put an oyster in my mouth, she picked up one end of the orange snake and circled it about us, then did the same with the other end of the snake. She was making the pillow-circle smaller around us, fencing us in, together. She sat down in front of me, picked up a strawberry and fed it to me. When I had finished eating it, she leaned over, brushing the soft skin of her cheek against mine. I could smell a faint and delicate aroma of flowers and pine; she had perfumed herself. She put her full lips on mine and kissed me slowly. I knew I was in the middle of a sensuously terrific experience many people would kill for.

I was dead in the kiss. I felt nothing. I admired the kiss, the way she kissed, the wonderful mouth she had, the lovely skin, the extraordinary scenario she had created. But I felt nothing. She knew it and sat back.

"I'm sorry," I said. "I think I had better leave."

"Oh no, oh no," she said softly, "you mustn't leave." Her eyes were wet. "Stay and eat and talk to me. Relax. You will feel better later."

The walls, shining with the last light of day, were closing in on me. Perhaps the orange-snake coil would get smaller and smaller until it began to advance up my torso, stopping my breathing.

"I *am* sorry, but I'm going to go," I said, and I got up, stepped over the orange pillow, got my coat from the closet, and left quickly. She did not turn around, but sat very still, facing the tray and the corner where I had been resting my back.

As I rode down the elevator of the high-rise midtown apartment building, I felt like a long-shipwrecked Martian who yearns desperately to be part of earth society, but is always excluded by his strange looks and ways. Finally, an earth woman takes pity on him and draws him close and he learns that not only is he unpleasant for them, but they are unpleasant for him. He will be alone forever. Had I been too hasty? Maybe I would have felt better had I hung around for more strawberries and wine. Maybe she'd come on too strong, too soon. I could have told her that and given her a chance to back off. But I had left because I could not have stayed another minute.

I fought off guilt: I had treated her badly.

On the other hand, she had scared the shit out of me.

The rest of the tale is not pretty. She fell madly in love with me, or so she said, pursued me aggressively and at length, and, eventually, I had to be cruel to get her to leave me alone. I was not anxious to repeat the experience.

SOMETHING DIFFERENT was happening with Donna. I liked her and desired her. It was not a project.

But the Carmina episode had made me cautious. Also conscience-stricken. Hitting on students or letting them hit on you was not a good idea. Unethical even. We had brought that point home to men, hadn't we? I put off any expression of my desire for Donna to the end of term.

For her part, Donna always behaved with good-student propriety.

For the class's last session, I invited everyone to my apartment for drinks. Donna stayed to the last and remained to chat pleasantly with me alone. She talked about her day job, the strain between her and her immigrant parents, why she still lived there anyway, and how it felt to be in the closet in the Italian community. She seemed sensitive and sensible beyond her years, which I had put at 25 or so. I invited her to have coffee with me after work the following week; she smiled and said yes.

We met downstairs from the office where she worked, had coffee in the café across the street, and small-talked.

"I have to meet a friend," she said after an hour. I suppose I showed my disappointment, because she said, "Oh, had you wanted to talk longer? I didn't want to take up too much of your time, I thought you must be very busy."

"I am sometimes," I said, flattered. "But you are modest. You're very interesting to talk to, and pleasant to be with. I'd like to talk with you some more."

"I'd like that very much," she said.

"Perhaps you would come to dinner at my place next week."

"I would," she said. "I would like that." We looked shyly and, I thought, knowingly, at each other.

SHE WAS ON TIME. I had cooked simply, but well. *Pasta prima vera*. I hadn't overcooked the fusilli, the broccoli were *al dente*, the white sauce was not too thick, and the parmesan was freshly grated.

"*Molto buono*," Donna said softly, using Italian words for the first time in my presence. "*Molto buono*," she repeated, looking up at me and smiling.

It dawned on me that I was presenting pasta to a young woman whose mother probably made it fresh all the time and spent eight hours over the sauce, making it from scratch, just right. I felt stupid, then stupidly delighted at the compliment because, after all, she should know. And I was glad I had not made tomato sauce. I liked to cook well when I cooked, which was not often, but nothing would make me spend eight hours over a stove, stirring, adding, tasting, and stirring.

We talked about what it was like to try to make a living as an artist, whether it was worth it, what one might do instead. She talked about being lesbian, when she knew she liked girls in a special way (age nine), when she had her first romantic experience (13), and how she felt about men (nothing, really).

"I have been attracted to women sometimes in my life," I said, "but never had a...." I looked for the right word. "... a successful experience. I feel attracted sexually, I feel it here." I put my hand below my breasts and looked at her. She nodded, smiled slightly. "But something happens, something happens later, or, something does not happen, maybe that's what I should say, something does not happen. Things do not go the way I feel at first it would be nice for them to go." I looked foolishly and hopefully at her, she who knew herself, was so calm and self-assured. "Shit, I'm confused about my sexuality."

"I know," she said.

"You do?" I asked. "How do you know?"

"You have it about you. A lot of desire, strong desire, with nowhere to go with it. Or you haven't found where to go with it. You have a lot of sadness about that."

"You're right," I said. "You're perceptive."

"I don't know if I'm perceptive. I like you, I've watched you a lot, and thought about you a lot. Maybe you know that."

"I hoped that."

We were both suddenly quiet, spearing fusilli, sipping wine, not looking at each other.

I broke the silence. "I was attracted to you when you first came to class. But I had a...." Again, I was looking for the right words. "I had a messy involvement with a student once before, and I have a personal rule now not to get involved with students. My rules say it might be okay once the class is over. But I'm not sure it is. There's something about power between us that maybe is not fair to you. I don't know. And I'm a confused person about, about sex. Maybe that's not fair to you either."

She spoke in her gentle voice and considered words. "I have a girlfriend," she said, "a steady girlfriend. We are having some difficulties, but are trying to work them out."

"Oh," I said, feeling better. "I'm glad, I guess. You understand why I'm glad."

"I do," she said. "That's why I told you that. It's the truth, too. I also like to be fair."

"What kind of trouble are you having?"

"I've wanted to be monogamous, and she has not."

"Are you in love with her?"

"I have been. For a long time. A few years. Since university."

"You sound like you're not sure any more."

"I'm not sure. She hurts me. She doesn't seem to care. I don't like that. I like to be treated kindly."

"Sounds healthy to me," I said.

"So one thing I have begun to think is that I should not sit around and be hurt while she fools around."

"And so you are thinking about fooling around, too."

"In a way. I guess so," she said, then spoke abruptly, uncharacteristically, her voice higher and faster than usual. "But that's not why I'm *here*. I just really like you. I liked you all through class. It was great to find out you liked me, too. I never expected it. It was exciting." And now she stopped, embarrassed. "But don't worry. I don't have a big *crush* on you or anything. I won't be hurt. I'm okay. I'm a big girl," she said, sounding like a pre-teen.

"Okay," I said, "but I'm unstable, I'm warning you.

Perhaps I need to be... trained, slowly, gently, a little at a time. I don't know."

"Whatever happens, we will be friends, okay?"

"Yes, that's what I want. I like you as a person. I don't want to just use you. I don't want something unpleasant to happen."

She smiled at me. We finished our wine and went to sit on the sofa. "I'd like to smoke a joint," I said. "Dope relaxes me."

"Okay," she said.

We smoked the joint. I was very nervous. We smoked another one. I felt better. I liked having her sit next to me on the sofa. We sat sideways, so we could look at each other's faces. She did not have that wild, domineering energy Carmina had, nor did she look like she might crumble at my touch or melt at my words, the flip side of the demanding Carmina. She held her own. I felt safe with her.

She took my hand and stroked each finger, tracing the lines of the bones and veins. She moved closer to me and put her arm around my shoulder. With her other hand, she brushed the hair from my eyes and brought her face close to mine. She kissed me softly, briefly, on one corner of my mouth, then on the other corner, and then in the middle.

"I like you a lot," she said. Her voice was low, whispery.

"I like you, too." I felt awkward, but what she was

doing was pleasant. It felt affectionate, her skin was good on mine. I felt young, younger than her, much younger.

She stood up, took my hand, and pulled me gently up from the sofa, and led me to the bedroom. We lay down on my bed on our sides, facing each other. She brushed the hair from my face, as she had done on the sofa, and stroked my cheek. She is very nice, I thought, but I began to feel dizzy, then stiff, like the fluid around my joints was gelling and hardening. My sense of how her body was like mine, the breasts like mine, the nipples that might touch nipples, the pubic hair and the vaginal juices, how they might mix, suddenly it all made me scared, like I might vanish into her same-shaped body. I did not want to be in bed with someone whose body was like my body. Why was that? I did not know.

"Donna," I said. "I need to rest. I think I need to stop."

"Oh," she said, her voice easy, kind, disappointed. "Okay."

I felt guilty and rotten, but I also felt sick. I couldn't continue.

"I'm really sorry, Donna. I'm sorry. I don't know if it's genetic interference or mental disease. Shit."

She was getting her composure. "Look," she said, "it's okay. It's not like we didn't talk about this. You were straight with me. I took a chance, but I knew what could happen. It's okay. I'll be all right." I must have looked very downcast, because she patted me on the head, as though I were a child, and said, "It's not the end of the world."

"Okay," I said. "Thanks for being how you're being. I won't do this to you again. It's not fair. It's hard on you."

"It's a bit hard," she conceded.

"I'll make some tea?"

"Good idea," she said. She got up, went off to the bathroom, and washed her face.

This tale does not end ugly and is easy to tell. Donna and I stayed friends, but didn't go to bed (or couch) again. We talked on the phone and went out sometimes to eat. She made it up with her girlfriend for a while (her encounter with me did serve to spark some jealousy and I was grateful it had not been a total loss for her). Monogamy held sway for a year or so. Her girlfriend fell off the wagon into an affair. Donna broke it off, telling her lover it was not the kind of relationship she wanted. She moved to another city and, from time to time, I get a postcard or a phone call, solicitous, warm, from a woman with a sure and clear voice.

BRIAN'S DREAM / ARLA'S FANTASY

HE SAT SMOKING A CIGARETTE and wondered about the strange noise he was hearing. Then he realized it was a tiny woman in his ear, having an orgasm.

I wish I had six cocks, he said to the woman in his ear, one for each of your orifices. She sat counting the holes in her body and told him he'd need more.

"What is it about love, about wanting to love again?" the little woman in his ear asked loudly, in the dream.

This woke Brian up and he said, out loud, "What is it about love? About wanting to love again?"

This woke up the regular-sized woman sleeping next to him in bed. "What?" Arla said, "what did you say?"

"I said," he said, "what is it about love, about wanting to love again?"

"Oh," Arla said, "that's easy. The second time around your tolerance has grown. You are in danger of understanding things to death. Including your own death."

Brian said, "Nice moon out tonight," and fell back asleep. "Hello," he said, in the dream, "hello, you in my ear. How many cocks will I need?"

"Seven," she said, "the magic number—seven."

"When will you come out of my ear?" he said. "When will you come out so I can see you, little woman?"

"In due time," she said. "I'm so happy here. The outer ear is perfect. I like resting my shapely bum against it. It's warm and secure in the curves of the ear. I like being naked in your ear. Why do you have to see me? Can't you feel me in your ear? Can't you feel my beautiful bum on the curve of your ear? And my lovely full breasts and erect nipples rubbing against the skin of your ear?"

But Brian couldn't feel anything. He could only hear this warm, sexy woman's voice in his ear. His imagination, as you might imagine, was going wild.

"I want to see you," he whined.

"That's not possible," she said. "And don't get any funny ideas," she continued. "Remember your mother told you never to put anything smaller than your elbow in your ear."

But Brian felt himself at the mercy of the forces of nature. He couldn't help himself. The little finger on his right hand began to uncurl from its comfortable fist. He raised his hand to his ear and probed it with his pulsing finger. His fingertip touched tiny beautiful breasts with tiny, hard beautiful nipples. He moved his finger slowly against the tiny beautiful bum.

His heart was pounding. His finger was stiff and sweaty.

"Don't do it, Brian," the little woman said. "You'll be sorry. Seriously. You will really be sorry."

But Brian couldn't control himself. You know what I mean: a stiff little finger has no conscience. He was overwhelmed. He slid his finger down her beautiful bum and felt the tiny warm and wet place between her legs. He wiggled his finger and gave a little push.

Pop.

She was gone.

"Oh no, what have I done?" Brian moaned.

"Hi, Brian," said the voice of the little woman. But the warm and sexy voice had become cold and bitchy.

"Where are you?" he moaned.

"In your inner ear," she said. "I warned you. I told you you'd be sorry. But you let your finger do the thinking. Tch, tch, tch."

"What should we do?" he asked.

"Don't worry, honey. I'm just gonna stay here and describe my tiny beautiful body to you until you die. I told you that you'd be sorry. You shoulda listened." Her voice had gone nasal and whiny, with a definite Brooklyn twang.

"You spoke so nicely to me when you were sitting in my outer ear," Brian sniffed.

"I was within reach of that little finger then," she said.

"I'll fix you," he said, "I'll wake up."

"Yes," she said, "but you will sleep again."

Brian woke up and turned his body to the woman next to him in bed. "Do you love me, Arla?" he said, waking her up.

"Yes," she said.

"I can't hear you," he said. "I have a woman in my ear."

"What?" she said, "what?"

"Nothing," he said. "Just a bad dream."

"Well, I do love you," Arla said.

"Thanks," he said. "If you hear me talking in my sleep tonight, just wake me up and tell me you love me."

"Sure," she said. "I'd do anything for you, you know that."

"You're a good woman," he said. He turned on his side and was soon snoring.

Arla cuddled up to him and put her mouth to his ear. "Hey," she whispered, "keep up the good work."

THE RUNNER

A NOVELLA

She is the redhaired runner beat up by the cops. She runs along the Toronto lakeshore at four in the black August morning. When the cops stop her, she shouts at them and takes off. They give chase in their car, catch her, and pound her with their fists until they are tired.

She was always off the beaten track, but now she's going over the edge. Realizing that she hates everyone in the world, she gets pregnant and has a son whom she loves without respite. She is split like the Grand Canyon. Her child is perfect and she has no bad feelings about him. Adults are suspect. They oppress and damage her.

ONE

THE PARKDALE PARENT AND Child Drop-In Centre was dominated by a clique of vegetarian Buddhist pacifists on welfare who were always angry at each other.

"Talk about holier-than-thou," Felicia was saying to Arla. "Susan is so arrogant, I mean she really excels in arrogance. Buddhists are supposed to be humble and modest. But all you hear from her is how she's off dairy products, and then she asks you, are you still eating cheese and eggs? And then she tells you all the ways she's learned to prepare soy. I mean, who asked? Now she's got a new name. I can't even pronounce it. The spiritual leader of the temple gave her a name, which means she's reached some level of spiritual wisdom. Really he just wants her to keep living at the temple because he needs the rent.

And she is always proselytizing people, you know. Real Buddhists don't proselytize."

As an admitted eater of meat and non-practitioner of yoga, Arla was often the person the feuding Buddhists came to in order to complain about each other. Felicia spoke to her frequently. Arla was neutral territory. She was so far off the path of spiritual wisdom, she was out of competition.

Arla liked Felicia a lot, despite Felicia's wide mood swings. Felicia wanted badly to be saintly and would give it a stab for a few days, then lapse into deep depression, hating herself for her failures and being angry at all the people she had helped who did not appreciate her and were just using her. Felicia was at her best during the transition period when she was emerging from depression and before giving another bash at sainthood. Arla found her easy to talk to at these times, warm, good-humoured.

Felicia finished venting her anger about Susan, and lapsed into a monologue about the philosopher Gurdjieff. Her dark brown eyes were steady above her olive cheekbones, her thick and wavy black hair wild around her face. She concluded her speech with a pointed look at Arla. "Those who don't realize this won't be saved when the catastrophe comes." Arla returned the gaze, her blue eyes steady, her long, brown hair flat against her head. She was about to make a crack about not proselytizing, when the redhaired runner strode up to them.

ARLA HAD MET the redhaired runner at the centre the previous week. The runner was wearing a long-sleeved white blouse, blue vest, ankle-length cotton print dress with small blue and white flowers, and white socks in white running shoes. She was short and apparently slim, but it was hard to tell what exactly might be under the flowing garments that covered her almost entirely. Arla didn't know yet that the runner had red hair because it was all pinned up and tucked under a white cotton hat with a brim in front. The runner's hands and face looked very naked; Arla wondered if she carried gloves and, perhaps, a fan.

At first, the runner didn't talk to anyone. She walked around quietly, holding her infant son. He had a large, bald head and stared at his mother's pale face with big, unblinking brown eyes. The runner didn't put him on the bare wooden floor to play nor did she sit down or stand still. She just kept circling the large church basement slowly, looking at things, but not meeting anyone's eyes. She paused to let her son stare at the bright red and blue toys in the play corner; when he reached for one, she moved on, circling past the secondhand flowered sofa, orange fading to brown, the bright green easy chair with white stuffing leaking from its cushion, and the damaged straight-backed chairs strewn here and there. No one went up to her to say hello. Everybody at the centre had their problems and they weren't keen on getting an earful of someone else's.

After a while, the runner stopped her circling to listen to some women talking about their welfare cheques. She kept her eyes averted, but nodded when someone complained about a caseworker.

"You must be a new member of the welfare mothers' contingent here," Arla said in her bright and loud voice.

The runner's face reddened. "I guess I am," she said, almost inaudibly.

"Well, another welfare mother is always welcome around here," Arla continued, her voice still loud, and laughed. "How old is your...boy? girl?"

"Eight months old. It's a he."

"What's his name?"

"Hrothgar."

Arla recognized the name of one of the kings in *Beowulf*, but decided not to remark, since the woman's voice trembled when she uttered her son's name. Touchy, better be careful, thought Arla. That's what happens when you name your son Hrothgar, imagine the fun he'll have later in school.

"What do you do besides take care of your son?" Arla asked, adding quickly, "Of course, that's a full-time job by itself. Who has time for anything else?"

"I run," said the woman, and paused a minute. "But since I've had my son I haven't had time." She turned away from Arla, walked across the room, sat down on the flowered sofa, and began nursing the baby.

"Done it again," Arla said to herself out loud.

Arla saw the runner in the local supermarket the next day. The two women were at the fruit counter pressing pears with their fingertips to find the ripe ones. The runner had no hat on and her beautiful head of long, full, red hair swept down her back and around her shoulders. Arla didn't recognize her at first. The runner's manner was completely different. She seemed relaxed in the supermarket, a place of ephemeral relationships where people could meet each other's eyes and speak, without thinking about the consequences.

"Is there any fruit on special today?" Arla asked her.

The woman looked up pleasantly at the taller, darker woman addressing her. Arla saw that she had light green eyes with small dark centres and was quite striking. "The Valencia oranges are cheap today," she said, "but my son doesn't like them. He only likes pears and bananas."

Arla looked at the baby in the shopping cart and recognized Hrothgar. "Hey, don't you go to the drop-in centre?" she asked. The runner started.

"Oh, sometimes, I go to the centre sometimes," she said, and dropped her glance to the floor. Then she looked up shyly at Arla, met her eyes for a moment in recognition, then turned back to the pears. "Can't find any ripe ones," she said, her hands suddenly darting from pear to pear.

"No, they'll have to stand outside and ripen a while,

I guess," said Arla, drawn back to the pears by the runner's movements. "But some of the bananas are ripe, if you need some ripe fruit for Hrothgar today."

The runner looked up gratefully. "Yes, Hrothgar hasn't had any ripe fruit today. I think he's constipated now."

"Where do you live?" Arla asked.

"Oh...not too far from here," she said.

"I'm just a few blocks away myself. Did you ever think of doing some exchange babysitting?"

The runner picked up her son protectively. "Oh, I don't know. I haven't had anyone else look after Hrothgar. I'm not sure," she said. She put him back in the shopping cart, took her white hat out of her pocket, put it on her head and started tucking her thick red hair into it.

"Maybe the four of us could visit together first and see how we feel about it," Arla said. "I don't get out much. Do you?"

"No... not much."

"Also I paint and now I can only paint at night, what with Sam up and about in the daytime. I'd like to do some painting in the morning. I work better in the morning. And the light's good," Arla said.

"Well...I'll think it over," the runner said.

"You like to go running, don't you? You could run while I watch Hrothgar."

"Oh...oh...okay... I would like to do some running,

I guess. It's been a long time since I did any running. I won the Toronto marathon two years ago." She said the last sentence quickly, rushing it out and turning red.

"No kidding," said Arla, "that's great."

The runner turned to leave, then turned back abruptly. "What sort of painting do you do?" she asked Arla.

"Oh, I'm into new realism, I guess. I keep starting a series of self-portraits but I'm having a lot of trouble with them. Sometimes I don't think I'll be able to do the series as long as my parents are alive," said Arla. The runner took a few steps backward and rubbed her forehead with her fingertips.

"That's a terrible thing to say, but I can't help feeling that way. It's like that film, that Woody Allen film, *Interiors.* Did you see it?" Arla didn't stop to wait for the runner's answer. "Great film—it's really his best. Too bad it got dumped on by reviewers. It was his first straight film, you know, and they couldn't stand him making a film that wasn't funny, because he never had before. Now, they're more used to it. So anyway, the woman in the film, the one who can't get it together at all, well, when her mother commits suicide, she feels released, and she starts writing like crazy. But her two other sisters, they were very active before the mother's death, one's an actress, and the other's a writer, and they get all blocked by the mother's death. Of course, I don't feel like watching any of Allen's stuff these days. I mean not since he shacked up with his stepdaughter. Shit. I mean, it's the late Woody Allen, as far as I'm concerned. But it's really interesting—the effect of your parents on your work, you know what I mean?" Arla didn't wait for an answer, but took a quick breath and continued. "But my painting's going okay. I've been doing a lot of work in the last few months. I got some grants, which is good because you know what welfare is like, and I had a show this year and actually sold a couple of paintings. And I've got a lover at the moment, so I can't really complain. I'm painting, eating, and getting laid a couple of times a week. My son is happy and healthy. So I've got my basics, you know what I mean?"

Arla was about to continue without waiting for an answer, but the runner interrupted her.

"What's your lover like?" she asked, stepping back suddenly from the pears and pressing her hands together in front of her. The runner looked back at the pears, her face full of regret at having asked a second question. They might be at the pears forever.

"My current lover? Oh, he's a soft-core sadist with an underwear fetish." Arla laughed a short, hard laugh. "He's a bit strange, but he's okay. He's an actor, out of work at the moment. So he got a job at Metro Zoo, doing grounds maintenance and stuff like that. I guess being near all those animals gets to you after a while." Arla laughed at her own joke and then noticed that the runner was slowly edging away and that she, Arla, was talking to the nearby shoppers, who were quite interested.

"Hey, wait a minute," Arla called to the runner, who kept moving. Arla walked up to her. "Look, here's my phone number." She tore a small piece of paper in half, writing a number on one piece. "What's yours?"

The runner hesitated, then took the blank piece of paper extended toward her. "I guess I would like to do some running," she said and wrote her number down and gave it back to Arla.

AND HERE THE RUNNER was again, arriving at a good time, too, Arla thought. She was tired of sparring with Felicia about enlightenment.

"Hi!" the runner said brightly and both Arla and Felicia started. She was completely out of character. "How are you doing?" she continued in the same breezy tone.

Felicia and Arla exchanged wary glances. Felicia said, "Good. I feel good today. How about you?"

"Oh, really good," the runner said.

Arla noticed that the runner was not holding her son. She had never seen her without the baby in her arms, except for that time in the supermarket when he was next to her in the shopping cart. The runner had not called Arla about that babysitting exchange.

"Where's Hrothgar?" Arla asked. Felicia looked at Arla about to say, *Who?*, but Arla knitted her brows purposefully and Felicia kept quiet.

The runner watched this exchange, took a deep breath, and said, "Hrothgar? Oh, *Hrothgar's* right over there." She repeated her son's name slowly and loudly, looking seriously from Arla to Felicia and back to Arla. Suddenly she smiled broadly, in the bright and breezy way she had come over to say hi. "He's playing over there, with a little boy." They turned and saw the eight-month-old crawling around some chairs. An older child was playing peek-a-boo with the infant.

"That's Sam," Arla said, "that's my son."

"Oh, no kidding, that's great," the runner swept along. "What a nice little boy. How old is he?"

"Five," said Arla, smiling at her son. "He is a nice kid, isn't he? Don't know who he takes after, he's so easygoing and sociable. It's certainly not me or my ex-husband," Arla laughed.

The runner frowned slightly, moved back a step, then laughed, too. Three short laughs and a sudden silence. She tried to push out a few more laughs but coughed instead. "Maybe he takes after a grandparent," she said, trying to be part of Arla's joke, but speaking a bit too seriously.

Arla had expected to be reassured she was a friendly, pleasant person. "His grandparents on both sides are a drag, too," she said with an edge in her voice, "but my grandfather—you know, Sam's great-grandfather—they say he was easy to get along with."

"That's great," the runner said, still making an effort to have a conversation like anyone else.

Felicia had been standing by quietly, observing the exchange between Arla and the runner. She announced, "I'm not feeling well."

"Why, what's wrong?" asked Arla.

"Too much bad karma around here."

"Make yourself some camomile tea. That'll calm you down," said Arla. "It's too early in the day to be thinking about the imperfection of the universe."

"I'll make rosehip. Better to be fortified than calm," said Felicia.

Arla and the runner sat down on the sofa. The runner took another short, deep breath. "So let's get together soon and talk about this babysitting exchange," she said.

"Great. How about this afternoon? Are you busy?" asked Arla.

"No," said the runner. "Why don't you come by my place? I've just prepared a special tea of seven herbs, my own recipe. I'll make you some."

"Sure," said Arla.

T W O

THE WINDOWS OF THE RUNNER'S basement apartment were plastered with bronze plaques from races she had won. The beige walls were bare, except for one wall in the front room, which was entirely covered by a huge oil painting composed of 24 squares. Inside each square was an open mouth. Each set of lips was painted a slightly different shade of purple.

"That's quite a painting," Arla said to the runner.

"My husband did it. I mean my ex-husband."

"Yeah, I've got one of those, too," Arla laughed.

The runner winced.

"Eight years with the guy, can you believe it?" said Arla. "After I had my son I couldn't stand it any more. One baby at a time, you know what I mean? In fact that's

107

what I said to him when I asked him to leave and not come back. One baby at a time... "

"Do you like the painting?" the runner interrupted her.

Arla had hated the painting instantly. "It's really unusual," she said. "It's... " she hesitated, thinking about what to say.

"I don't like it either," the runner said abruptly and fell silent. She took a deep breath, but it didn't work, and she lapsed into the manner more familiar to Arla, turning her eyes to the floor.

"Tea, let's have some tea," Arla said, unconsciously mimicking the runner's bright tone of voice from the morning.

"Don't make fun of me," the runner said quietly.

"Oh. I didn't mean to. I... well, I was just trying to be cheerful," Arla said. She decided to change the subject. "Hrothgar's an interesting name. Where did you get it?" she asked. The runner's shoulders tensed and Arla realized it was exactly the wrong thing to say, just as she'd suspected earlier. Why had she forgotten?

"It's an old English name. My great-grandfather's brother was named Hrothgar. He became a famous doctor and nobody made fun of his name then," she said.

"I think it's a great name. I'd just never heard it before and wondered where you got it," said Arla, deciding not to say anything about King Hrothgar in *Beowulf*.

"Well, that's where I got it," the runner said stiffly.

Arla tried another subject. "Were you working before you had the baby?"

The runner's shoulders twitched and Arla thought
she had offended her again, but the anger in the runner's
eyes was not directed at Arla.

"I worked at the main library," said the runner. "Just
clerical work."

"Do you think you might go back there when
Hrothgar's older?" Arla asked.

"I can't. I got fired. And the union is blacklisting me
so I can't work in library jobs anywhere any more," the
runner said, adding quietly to herself: "They are. I know
they are. The fuckers."

"What happened?"

"It's a long story," the runner said. She paced the
floor and shook her head. Sometimes she stopped suddenly, bringing her hands together in front of her as she
had done at the pears, and was quiet for a moment. Then
she would resume. "My supervisor was a dyke. She
wanted me to go to bed with her. I know she did. Well,
I was cool to her. I made it clear that she wasn't getting
anything like that from me. I mean, I'm not a lesbian.
I'm not one of those people. So I made it clear that I
wasn't like that, and she made up a report on me, saying
I couldn't get along with my co-workers, and making up
a lot of stories."

"Did you ask for a hearing after you got fired?" Arla
asked.

"No. There's a lot of dykes down at the library, you know. What chance would I have? They were all against me. Lesbians are like that; they stick together."

Arla interrupted her. "There are lesbians down at the drop-in centre, you know."

"There are? Who are they?" The runner widened her eyes.

Arla was thinking of Harriet and Lisa, a lesbian couple with four small children from previous straight marriages. They were vegetarians, but didn't proselytize. Arla had no idea if they were Buddhists or not.

"Oh, I don't know," said Arla. "Florence, you know, the director, just mentioned to me that there were some lesbian mothers there. I don't remember why."

"Oh," said the runner, eyeing Arla with suspicion.

"I can't really agree with you, what you're saying," Arla continued in her friendliest manner. "Lesbians are pretty much like everyone else. Anyway, there probably aren't so many lesbians down at the library as you think there are."

The runner pressed her lips together. "Maybe you're a lesbian, too," she said.

Arla laughed. "I wish. I'm a failed lesbian actually. I've always wanted to be a lesbian. Women are much better company than men, don't you think?"

"I hate men," the runner said. "All they want to do is fuck."

"Well, I don't know about that—although fucking's

okay, I wouldn't want to put it down. That's always been my problem. I tried it with women, but it just didn't do it for me, you know what I mean?" Arla said casually, and suddenly thought she was talking too much, a rare feeling. She looked around the room. Behind the beige walls, an army of eyes and ears watched her and listened, led by their jumpy, driven, redhaired commando, at this moment delivering a pronouncement to the captured Arla.

"I don't think lesbians should be down at that centre. There should be another group for lesbians," the runner told her.

"I can't really agree with you," Arla said flatly, not sure what to say next, and thinking maybe she should leave and just forget the whole thing.

A burst of howling from the front room cut short the conversation. The two women went into the room. Hrothgar had crawled up to Sam and picked up one of his toy cars. Sam grabbed it back and Hrothgar fell over, banging his head on the floor. He lay there now, screaming, while Sam held on to his toys.

"Oh, Sam, what did you do? That's not nice." Arla's voice was harsh and Sam started to cry.

"Oh, hey," the runner said softly to Sam. "Don't cry. Hrothgar's okay. Look, he stopped crying." She picked up Hrothgar and brought him over to Sam. Sam glared at the infant and pushed away the hand that was again reaching for his toys. The runner stroked Sam's hair, saying softly, "It's nice to be gentle, like this." She took Sam's hand and stroked her son on the head with it, then let go of his hand. Sam's curiosity had been aroused and he put his hand on the infant's face carefully, feeling the nose and mouth, and then smiled at the runner.

Arla watched quietly. That was the right way to handle that scene. She ought to have done it that way. This woman was a little crackers all right, but she was good with kids.

Hrothgar had cheered up and was crawling back to the kitchen. Sam was playing with his toys again. "How about next week?" Arla asked. "You take my son on Tuesday, I'll take yours on Wednesday."

"Okay," said the runner, smiling at Sam and then looking up dubiously at Arla.

THREE

ARLA DROPPED SAM OFF at the runner's apartment
Tuesday morning. The runner had imposed a cheerful
attitude on herself and she smiled and chatted with Arla.
"What are you going to do with your day off?" she asked.

"I haven't had eight whole hours to myself in, I don't
know—it's been forever, I think. I'm going to glue
myself to a canvas. But first I'd like to take a long walk
down by the lake," said Arla.

"Sounds great. See you at six," the runner said with
her forced smile.

Sam seemed happy, drawing a picture of himself on
a wall the runner had designated for this purpose. He
briefly turned and looked anxiously at Arla as she kissed

the top of his head and went out the door. Then he resumed his work at the wall.

Arla walked toward Lake Ontario. At the spot where Springhurst Avenue curves sharply, gusts of warm August lake wind swooped down on her. The sudden change of atmosphere brought back an old feeling of openness, possibility. The wind grew stronger as she neared the lake.

It's really beautiful here, she thought. The sky is blue and wide, the gulls fly with such ease, the water seems to go on and on. Space and water. The last grace left with us. Arla walked across the wide grassy area. The old concrete walkway by the edge of the lake bulged and fractured with emerging clumps of grass.

A small girl played on the steps leading to the edge, collecting discarded paper cups, bottles, and cigarette butts. She threw them into the lake one by one, watching to see which way each thing would float. Arla was about to say, hey, don't do that, when she looked up and down the lake edge. Shards of white styrofoam bobbed between blackened spears barely discernible as plant growth. Pulverized bits of no longer identifiable garbage floated in scummy bubbles. What difference would a few butts make? Except to spoil the little girl's fun.

Arla suddenly remembered the time at the drop-in centre when the women had planned to go on a picnic and she had had a small run-in with Susan, Felicia's arrogant Buddhist. Everyone was rushing around trying to get food prepared, checking if there were paper plates, finding out who had cars or how to go by streetcar, and locating children. Arla remarked to Susan that preparations for the picnic were pretty chaotic and disorganized.

"It's not chaotic," Susan said, eyeballing Arla with her I-am-compassionate-let-me-help-you look. "Things are just developing organically."

"Yeah, well, volcanoes are organic, too, you know. Sometimes they explode and kill a million people. Sometimes nature fucks up," Arla snapped at Susan, who responded by giving a serene bow and backing up two steps. If Felicia hadn't told Arla once that this was how the students at the Buddhist temple were taught to respond to anger, Arla probably would have thrown something at Susan. Instead, she said, "Oh, all right. Let's get going. If you just tell me which organic cars we're using, Sam and I will be on our way."

Funny how people make this split between organic and artificial or between natural and unnatural, Arla thought now, looking at the polluted lake with its saintly blue cap of sky. Human beings are organic, right? And they're the ones who make this pollution and concrete. So isn't all this garbage and technology natural, some extension of nature? It's a murky way to think: natural, unnatural. Maybe I would feel better with words like "good" and "evil."

But Arla didn't feel better. It seemed a touch religious to her and she didn't like to think of herself as religious any more. That was okay when she was in school. She tried to think of other polarities that would make her feel comfortable with the combination of lake and concrete. Active, quiet. Beautiful, ugly. Healthy, sick. Maybe healthy, sick would work. You could think of certain things as abnormalities or deformities. Enough deformities and you had disease, enough disease and you had death.

Arla took in a deep breath, and let it out with a sigh and a groan, shaking her head.

The little girl turned away from her game. "What's the matter, lady, are you sick?" she asked.

Arla laughed. She had forgotten someone was there. "No, I'm okay. It's just..." Arla tried to come up with a reason for the groan. "I have to go to the bathroom and there's no toilet around here."

"There's no bathroom for a long ways," the little girl said. "I go in those bushes over there." She giggled, then looked at Arla to see if she was going to be scolded, but Arla was smiling at her. "No one can see you in there," the girl continued.

"Well, I guess that is a good idea," said Arla, walking over to the cluster of bushes. She went inside and crouched down to see how protected it was. Several people passed close by and didn't look her way. She stood up, pulled her blue jeans and white underwear down and crouched again, bending backwards a bit and supporting herself with one hand so as not to get pee on her socks and shoes. She listened to the sound of urine hitting dry leaves and spied on passersby, feeling successful and smart like when she was a kid and used to pee in the bushes in the park, so she wouldn't have to go all the way upstairs, and became expert at not being seen and not wetting her socks. She was eight or nine years old then, she guessed. After nine, self-consciousness had set in like a rusty bolt.

Arla finished peeing and shook herself to dry off. She stood, pulled up her underwear and jeans and walked back toward her apartment, waving at the little girl who grinned and waved back. The trees were in full, rich late-summer leaf and here and there people sat on their lawns enjoying the morning sun. Arla found herself feeling sociable.

Two teenagers who sat on the steps of a grey stone house did not respond to Arla's smile and hello. She remembered it was one of the halfway houses in the area. The Parkdale neighbourhood was a mix of working people, welfare recipients, petty criminals, artists and other bohemian types, and, lately, had become a dumping ground for victims of hospital budget cuts. Psychotics of various kinds who could, however, manage to say their names and find their way home to the same place every night were released from the hospital and sent to live in the surrounding neighbourhood.

The residents of the stone house Arla passed now were a little different. A friend of hers who worked at the local hospital said this place was for young people who had suffered partial brain damage because of a car accident, a doctor's mistake, or some other mishap. They had been normal before, and the theory was that taking them out of the hospital, out of an environment of disease, and putting them back into the neighbourhood, into a normal and healthy environment, would create the basis for a better readjustment to the world. There was a lot of emphasis placed on the correlation between a positive or happy mental attitude and the brain's physical ability to regenerate cells.

It's a nice theory, thought Arla, but the reason they don't say hello back is because they get so much shit from everyone in the area all the time. They're afraid when you say hello. Are you making fun? Are you going to shy away when you pass closely and see the way their eyes don't look in the same direction? Most of the people in the house seemed to have the same problem with their eyes. Arla wondered if they all had a similar type of brain damage or if some treatment they were receiving had a side effect on their eyes.

She remembered literally running into one of the house's inhabitants in the bank one day. She hadn't been looking where she was going and bumped into a nice-looking young man. "Sorry," she mumbled. He stopped and turned slowly around to her. He didn't turn his head toward her as a normal person might do; he turned his whole body around to face her.

"I'm sorry I bumped into you," he said slowly and

methodically, as though reading a script. "But I have a physical problem." He moved aside the hair on his right temple to show her. The temple was caved in. It looked like it had been crushed by a large blunt instrument a long time ago. The skin was smooth and unblemished. He pushed the hair back over the concave spot and continued. "I had an accident and it affected my vision and balance. I have no peripheral vision and sometimes I bump into things which are out of my line of sight." Taken aback by the prepared speech, Arla didn't say a word in response. He smiled very slightly and walked away.

She didn't see him as she passed the house now. There were three young people, two boys and a girl, sitting and talking to each other. She was well past the house and turned to look back. One of the girls waved briefly. Arla waved back and kept walking.

She got home and felt immensely relieved to get inside. She was comfortable here, in surroundings of her own making. The outside often made her feel discordant, ill. She had an impulse to draw all the curtains but told herself it was not the thing to do in the middle of the morning on a bright August day. She remembered the runner's windows, covered with plaques.

Arla made herself a cup of coffee and sat down with it in front of a bare canvas she had constructed the previous night. It was a large canvas and would cover most of a wall in her small apartment.

F O U R

"I HAD A DREAM ABOUT YOU last night, Felicia," Arla said, putting a bag of camomile tea in a cup of hot water.

"Wrong tea for the morning," said Felicia. "Better go for peppermint if you want to stay up."

"It takes a lot to put me to sleep, any time of day or night," said Arla, stroking Sam's head as he sat next to her on the floor with a colouring book. "I'm Toronto's leading insomniac."

"I'll have some tea, too," said the runner, who was standing next to Arla, holding Hrothgar. Since the two women had begun watching each other's children two weeks ago, the runner had stuck to Arla's side like glue when they were at the centre. Arla was flattered, but slightly uncomfortable.

"So what did you dream?" Felicia said.

"I dreamed that some people in the neighbourhood want to get rid of the crazies in the area," said Arla. "So they get together in a big group and they're walking down my street, because one of those halfway houses is there. And they're about to move on the house. Then a group of us from the drop-in centre happen to walk by with our kids. And someone says, 'There's too many of these welfare people around, too. Let's get them.' And someone else says, 'Just take the kids, then they can't get welfare.' And they start coming toward us. You're not with us, Felicia. But suddenly you appear behind the crowd, with your son, and you lift him in the air and say, 'Take him, take my son instead.' They all turn around. You put Dylan down and then you stretch out your arms in front of you and meditate. Dylan walks through the crowd, and it opens like the Red Sea when Moses gets there with the Jews. The people don't seem to know what to do. They all start going home. Then I woke up."

Felicia loved the dream. "You won't believe me," she said, her smile tolerant of Arla's failures of faith, "but that's like a vision I had during a meditation last week. Only in my vision the crowd was hunting seals, but right there in the middle of the street, not in Newfoundland or anything. And I offered Dylan for the life of a baby seal, and they all went home."

"No kidding," Arla said. "It's like Mary offering up Jesus to be crucified."

Felicia blanched. She was an ex-Catholic and her conversion to Buddhism had a few rough spots. "Mary didn't do that," she said.

"I know, I know. I'm saying it's *like* that, as *though* Mary had done that," Arla said.

"I wouldn't sacrifice Hrothgar for a seal," the runner said somberly.

"For christ's sake," Felicia muttered. "Don't be so damn literal."

"Compassion is the key to enlightenment, Felicia," Arla said, deadpan, then smiled gently, making amends.

Felicia glared at her. "There's too much bad karma around here. I don't think there's much I can do about it. Compassion can go so far. You two have to work out your bad karma on your own." She left them, went over to where her son was fingerpainting on the floor, and joined him in the paint.

"Felicia's a bit touchy, but she's okay," Arla said.

"She seems pretty grouchy and conceited for a Buddhist," the runner said. "And I thought Buddhists aren't supposed to go around recruiting people, like Catholics. Buddhists are only supposed to tell you if you ask."

"Yeah, right. Well, I don't know who's the best Buddhist in this place, but Felicia's okay as people go. She'll come through if you need her. That's probably why I had that dream about her. She'd probably do it, what she did in the dream. I don't mean she'd give up her son like that, but she might figure out a way to get the mob to go away. And she wouldn't sacrifice her son for any seal either," said Arla.

"I don't like her," said the runner.

"You don't seem to like anyone," Arla said.

"I know. I don't want to be that way, you know, but that's how I am," said the runner.

"It's probably just a matter of time before some of that comes my way," Arla said.

"The tea's getting cold," the runner said, and handed Arla her cup. "You want to have dinner at my place today?"

"Okay," Arla said.

The centre was closing and Arla and the runner gathered up their sons and walked to the runner's apartment.

"Are beans and rice and vegetables okay?" the runner asked.

"Sure. Are you a vegetarian, too?" Arla asked.

"Yes."

"Are you a religious vegetarian or a healthy vegetarian? Or just broke?"

"I don't like to talk about it much," the runner said.

"Hey, maybe you're the only real Buddhist down at the centre." Arla laughed.

"If you don't like beans and rice we can try something else," the runner said.

"Take it easy, I'll change the subject. Beans and rice sound great, really," said Arla. "So talk to me about running. You don't talk much about it, you know. I never shut up about painting. How'd you start running? How do you feel when you're running?"

At last Arla had found a question the runner liked. She said, easily, "I feel good. I'm by myself. I feel clean. I like the wind. I like to feel my skin in the air. I like to be fast. I like to be faster than everyone else, better than everyone else. When I'm really running, no one can run faster than me." She stopped, embarrassed. Her hands began to shake.

"That's beautiful, that's really beautiful," Arla rushed to say. "Where's the best place to run, what's the best time of day?"

The runner's hands stopped shaking. "Down by the lake's the best place," she said tentatively. "So much space and water, so much air, so much room. Down by the lake at night is really best, just before the sun comes up." She stopped abruptly again and was quiet.

"That sounds great. I guess you can't run at night now, what with Hrothgar. Did you do that a lot, before you had the baby?"

"I did, but then I stopped."

"Why?"

"I had a bad experience," the runner said.

"Really? What happened?" Arla looked up. The runner was quiet and seemed deep in thought. "Are you okay?"

"Yeah, I'm okay. I just get upset remembering what

happened. I don't know if I want to talk about it. I get upset thinking about it. I don't talk about it much. I talked to a lawyer once."

"Maybe you'll feel better if you tell me," Arla said, not sure any more if she wanted to hear. The runner was pressing her hands together at the fingertips and flexing them like two spiders. Arla didn't want to bear the responsibility of listening to the story. But it was too late to back out.

"The cops stopped me once and beat me up," the runner said.

This wasn't anything like what Arla expected to hear. She wasn't sure what she expected—maybe suddenly being afraid of the night, maybe trouble from some guys.

"Why? Why did they do that?" Arla asked.

"Cops do stuff like that," the runner snapped.

"Listen, I hate cops as much as the next guy, but they have a job to protect, so usually they at least invent an incident or something," Arla said.

The runner looked angrily at Arla. "I don't think they worry too much about their jobs. Anyway, the guys they're working for are cops, too. They don't seem to worry too much about people getting beat up, as long as they're not important people. They just beat me up, just like that. You want to know why? Because they liked it, that's why." The runner was raising her voice and her face was getting flushed.

Arla couldn't help thinking there must have been

some provocation, but she didn't want the runner to get more agitated than she already was. "You have a point. So what exactly happened?"

"I was running along the lake where I usually run. It was really late; it must have been around four in the morning. But I had run that late a number of times before and nothing happened. So this time I'm running along and these cops pull up in their car and tell me to stop. One of them leans out the window and says, 'What are you doing here? Why are you out so late?' I told him I was just running and that he was interrupting my run, and I took off. They drove after me and got out of their cars and dragged me into the back seat and started punching me. They punched me up pretty bad." The runner's face was very red and her voice had become high and loud.

Arla was quiet. She was remembering the story about all the dykes at the library. "What happened with the lawyer?" she asked.

"They're as bad as the cops. That legal clinic, you know, the one the centre uses, these student lawyers, they're all patting each other on the back about helping the poor, but all they care about is themselves. They don't want to help anyone who really has a problem. They don't want to get mixed up in a case which isn't going to get them some glory. They're self-centred, egotistical stars, that's all," said the runner.

"What happened exactly with the lawyer?" Arla asked again.

"She listened real sympathetically, and then called me back a week later and said she was unable to handle the case. She dropped me just like that. No explanation."

"That's weird. I've dealt with that legal clinic and they were really helpful," Arla said.

"Are you calling me a liar?"

Arla had begun to feel there was a problem with the runner's grasp on reality. "No, it just seems like there's some things you're not telling me," Arla said.

"Why should I tell you? You'll just say 'that crazy lady,' like everyone else. 'That crazy lady is imagining things again,'" said the runner and began to cry.

Arla didn't know what to do and just let the runner cry. She stopped crying after a while, and started fixing the vegetables. She didn't bother to rinse her face or even wipe her eyes with the back of her hand, but stood there smudged and drippy, handling the zucchini.

"I've been eating mostly vegetarian stuff lately, too," said Arla, "but only because I'm broke."

The runner nodded. "It does save money, doesn't it?" she said, and turned to Arla with wet, red eyes and that sudden, forced smile she put on from time to time. Christ, that smile is strange, Arla thought. It's like one of those edible wax mouths the kids buy at Hallowe'en.

FIVE

ARLA LAY ON HER BACK, looking at the ceiling. "That was a good fuck," said Brian, also on his back. He leaned toward her on one elbow. "Your ass looks so great sliding out of those black panties."

"Where's my T-shirt?" Arla said. She found it on the floor and pulled it over her head.

"Something wrong?" Brian said.

"I'm not in the mood to talk about my ass. Want a drink?" she asked.

"Okay." He held her underwear up to his face and inhaled loudly, for her benefit. Arla turned her back on him and walked half-naked to the kitchen. She filled two glasses with ice and Canadian Club. Brian had gotten into the habit of staying over one or two nights on the weekend. They called in pizza or Chinese food, had sex for a couple of hours, talked, fell asleep, and he went home the next afternoon. They both felt that more sex during the week would be nice. That might have brought them closer together, however, and this was the last thing either of them wanted. If Arla's slogan was "one baby at a time," Brian's was "familiarity breeds contempt."

Arla handed Brian his drink and sat down on the bed with hers. There was a knock on the front door. "Who the hell is that at 11:30 at night?" Arla said. Brian shrugged. More knocking. Arla pulled on her jeans and went to the door. "Who is it?" she asked in her least friendly voice.

"Me."

Arla recognized the runner's voice and opened the door. She was standing there, her face locked into that weird smile, Hrothgar resting on her left hip. "Hi," she said.

"Hi," Arla said stiffly. "It's pretty late to be out walking. What's up?"

"Not much," the runner said, walking past Arla into the living room. "Okay if I come in?" She didn't wait for an answer. "Hrothgar and I needed to get out for a while. I haven't seen you in two days. Thought I'd drop in and say hello."

She knows damn well Brian stays over Saturday night, Arla thought. "Brian's here," she said, "we've just been screwing. We're just barely finished." She made a point of speaking in the loud voice the runner hated.

"Oh, that's nice," the runner said with her big smile. She put Hrothgar down, took off her sweater, and straightened the collar on her white cotton shirt. "It's a bit chilly for an August night," she said. "Can I have a cup of tea?"

Arla tried out a pointed stare. The runner looked back with wide, steady eyes. Arla saw that she knew exactly what she was doing and had no intention of going away peacefully, not this minute anyway.

"Okay," Arla said. "Brian and I are having a drink in bed. Why don't you join us?"

"Sure," said the runner.

Arla made another drink and they went into the bedroom. Brian was lying on the bed naked, smoking a cigarette. He pulled the sheet up to his waist. "Hey," he said, "how about a little warning?"

"Sorry, Brian," Arla said.

Brian looked down at his half-naked body against the white sheets, then up again at the two women, slowly, taking in their legs, breasts, and then their faces. He grinned broadly.

"Hi," he said, "hi! You must be Arla's friend from the centre. I've heard so much about you and Hoh-gar. Yeah. C'mon in. Have a seat." He gestured to the bed.

"Thanks for saving me the intro, Brye," said Arla.

Looking at the runner, she said, "Yeah, sure, make yourself at home."

The runner smiled at Brian, met Arla's eyes for an instant, then sat on the edge of the bed near the sheeted ghosts of Brian's feet. She didn't correct his mispronunciation of her son's name.

Arla remained standing. "Okay, you guys," she said. She slowly removed her T-shirt and jeans, keeping her eyes on the runner, who reddened and sipped her drink. "Hey, ma, no underwear," Arla said, climbing back into bed, crawling between the runner sitting on the edge, and Brian, propped up on one elbow by the pillows, his lower body long under the sheets. She knelt next to him at the head of the bed, puffed up some pillows and sat against the headboard, bringing her knees up to her chest and circling her arms around them. "Oh dear," Arla said, in mock absentmindedness, and pulled a section of the sheet over her legs and exposed crotch.

Brian was delighted. He could hardly wait to see what would happen next.

What happened next was the runner opened her shirt and gave the baby her breast. Instead of unbuttoning the first few buttons as she usually did, she undid them all.

"You have nice breasts," Brian said, his grin widening. The runner didn't fasten any buttons.

"Cool it, Brian," Arla said.

"Yours are nice, too, Arl'," Brian said and smiled at her nonchalantly, mocking. She frowned at him, but he kept smiling. "Poor Arla, always bites off more than she can chew."

"Don't talk to me in the third person," she said.

"Too bad I'm not a painter like Arla," he said to the runner. "I'd like to paint the two of you together. The Redhead and the Brunette."

"Oh brother. This is what happens to out-of-work actors. Any stage will do," she said to him.

"Tch, tch. Don't third-person me, Arl'," he said.

"Would you like to paint us with or without clothes?" the runner asked brightly, smiling at Brian. Arla looked at her in amazement. The baby had stopped nursing and lay in his mother's lap, playing with the buttons on her shirt. The shirt was wide open, showing two rosy redhead's breasts, the nipples glistening with drops of milk. The runner seemed to feel Arla's look and turned her eyes into it, defiantly.

"Well..." Brian paused a moment as though he were thinking about the runner's question. "Yes, without clothes would be better, I think, yes. The contrast in skin tone and hair would be so effective on canvas. Don't you think so, Arl'?"

"Oh, yeah, definitely. On the other hand, maybe you'd like a soft, kind of hazy approach, like Degas," Arla said, professorially, "only without the tutus." Her tone changed abruptly, becoming sharp, angry. "*Brian...*"

He interrupted her, taking up her professorial tone. "The fair, redheaded...*Woman with Child*. The darker, brooding woman... *The Artist.*" Brian paused and gazed off into the distance, making a sweeping motion with his arm to indicate titles. "One thing I'd like to do when I do this painting is pull your hair back behind your ears and tie it, very severe. Like this." He got up on his knees, letting the sheet fall off him, and turned to Arla, pushing her hair back from her face with his two hands and holding it behind her neck. He bent over to kiss her mouth, but she turned her face away.

"Leave me alone, Brian."

"How do you think *I* should wear my hair?" asked the runner, throwing another challenging sidelong glance at Arla.

Brian took his hands off Arla's hair and moved over to the runner. "Well, I think your face requires more softness. Maybe I'd push your hair behind the ear on one side, like this." He arranged her hair so that it fell over one shoulder, covering a breast. He moved back as though to study his work. Then he pushed the hair slightly, exposing the breast. The runner grabbed a fistful of sheet, but otherwise stayed still. She smiled at Brian.

"I think you should paint a long series of her purple mouth, like her ex-husband did," Arla said. The runner's face began to redden. Her shoulders came forward, hovering over her breasts.

Brian raised his eyebrows at Arla and sat back on the bed, off his knees. Arla stood up and put on her bathrobe. "That's enough. It's time for you to leave," she said to the bent red face and hair of the runner. She looked at Brian. "Maybe you should both leave."

The runner lost her composure. She started to button her shirt but her fingers were stiff and wouldn't grasp the buttons. "I'm sorry," she said and started to cry.

"Oh shit," said Brian. He lit a cigarette and went to sit in the kitchen, covering himself with the topsheet on the way.

The runner continued to cry.

"All right, it's no big deal. I'm sorry, too," Arla said, and then let the runner finish crying. "Well, look, I'll see you on Tuesday. You're taking Sam on Tuesday, remember?"

"Yes, okay," said the runner, fingering her shirt and not looking at Arla. She gathered up her things, picked up her son who had been playing happily on the bed, and went out the door without looking up. That was the way she looked the first time Arla had seen her, circling the drop-in centre.

Brian came to the bedroom door, sheet flung over his shoulder.

"You're really a prize asshole, Brian," Arla said.

"What do you mean?" he said, angry. "You got the whole thing going. I was just playing along. Don't start what you can't finish."

"That's clever. Do you have any more clever advice?" Arla said.

"Let's not make a big hassle out of it. She'll get over it. Forget it," he said, softening.

"As a matter of fact, she started the whole thing," Arla said. "Then she goes and freaks out. She's so fucking weird sometimes."

"She may have started it, but you jumped right on the bandwagon. And you're the one who freaked first, not her."

"It's a good thing I freaked early on. I can imagine what she would have done had it gone on longer," said Arla.

"Maybe you can't imagine. Maybe you don't know her that well," Brian said.

"Maybe you should try and get to know her better, and tell me how it goes. But don't come crying to me if you get a kick in the erection."

"Okay, okay. Look, I'm just kidding. I'm not even attracted to her, anyway. All I know is you start this whole thing and then give me shit for playing along. What you really wanted was for her to freak and go home when you took your clothes off. But she didn't, she just hung in there. So I played along, too. I guess that wasn't in your special personal program or something," he said, angry again.

"You didn't just play along, dear. You were positively creative."

"Thanks," he said, bowing.

"Sure I got mad. Too bad I took it out on her instead

of you. You can take it. I should have just asked her to leave in the first place."

"She's probably tougher than she's letting on," said Brian. "I wouldn't worry about it too much."

"Well, I don't think any of the performers deserve a medal for that little scene," Arla said. "Anyway, there is still something really strange about her. I mean she did come here hoping to make a scene. Maybe I was stupid to indulge her, but still... and you should hear the latest story she's been telling me about cops, she says these cops stopped her at night when she was running and..."

"Spare me," Brian interrupted her. "I'm tired. Tell me the one about 'the runner and the cops' another day." He made quotation-marks gestures with his hands.

"I think I'm going to stop this babysitting exchange with her," Arla said. "She's too weird."

"I think you should keep up the arrangement, Arl'," he said. "You need it for painting."

"You're just afraid I might put some pressure on you to help me watch Sam, that's all," said Arla.

Brian smoked his cigarette and didn't say anything.

"Let's go to sleep," Arla said.

"Okay," he said. He turned off the light and rolled over on his side with his back to Arla.

"Are you asleep?" she said after a minute. Brian was one of those people who fell asleep almost instantly. This always infuriated Arla, the chronic insomniac.

"Not yet," he said, "but I'd like to be soon."

"Maybe I should get her to go to some therapy or something," Arla said.

Brian said, "Aaah, she's just not getting laid enough."

Arla stared quietly at the rumpled sheets for a few minutes. "You really are an asshole, Brian, you know that? Next time they have a Prize Asshole contest somewhere, I'm going to put your name in," she said. But Brian was already asleep, snoring loudly. Arla continued, talking to the back of his head. "You're so hard-edge, Brian. In fact, you're sick. Maybe not sick exactly." She brought her hands together at the fingertips, like the runner, making a cathedral, or twin spiders. "It's more like you have something missing, like that guy I ran into in the bank who had a piece of his head missing. You fit right into the neighbourhood. I guess I fit in, too. How exactly I'm not sure. But something's going wrong with me. Something's off."

Arla awoke at seven to find Sam standing next to the bed. "My head hurts," he said.

"You've got a fever," she said, feeling his forehead. "Go back to bed and watch TV. I'll bring you some apple juice."

SIX

ARLA SAT IN FRONT OF THE BIG CANVAS. She had painted a grid, dividing the canvas into several dozen squares. In the top row were portraits of the runner's face. The expression changed from square to square.

It was late Sunday afternoon and Brian had left an hour ago. Sam was napping fitfully. His fever had gone down a bit but he was very congested. It looked like a good siege of flu was in store. Arla decided to keep him home until the fever was gone, and keep him out of contact with other children. It looked like a long, dull week indoors.

She called the runner. "Sam's sick," she said.

"Oh, that's too bad. I'm sorry to hear that." Neither of them mentioned the previous evening.

"I'm going to keep him home till he's better, so let's not exchange this week," Arla said. "Also, I don't think you should come by, because I don't want him giving anything to Hrothgar, or catching anything else, on top of what he's got. You know when kids are down at these centres a lot, they pick up germs all the time. Who knows what Hrothgar might bring here? And Sam will be really susceptible, being already sick."

"Oh... okay," the runner sounded suspicious. Arla felt too tired and harassed to worry about it.

"I've got to go. Sam's crying," Arla said.

"I don't hear him crying."

"I'll send you a tape recording," Arla said. "Talk to you later. Bye." She hung up the phone, and applied some purple to the mouth in the first portrait.

The week dragged by slowly. Arla was not used to Sam being cranky and restless. She felt irritable with him, then guilty. She painted furiously while he was napping, and this soothed her.

Despite being stuck in the house, she didn't feel like seeing anyone and called Brian and asked him not to come by until Sam was better. Then she unplugged the phone so everyone would stop bothering her.

I've got to get out of here for a while, Arla thought, one night toward the end of the week. I shouldn't leave Sam alone, but I've just got to get some air. I'll go out for 20 minutes. The building won't burn down in 20 minutes. Sam is sleeping, he'll be all right. I'll go nuts if I don't get out of here for a few minutes.

She went in to look at Sam asleep in his bed. "I'm going out for a few minutes, I'll be right back," she whispered to his sleeping body. He sniffled and turned over onto his stomach, one side of his face against the wrinkled sheet. Arla smoothed the sheet around his face and listened to his laboured breathing. "Shit," she said, louder, images of baby faces, their throats and nostrils sucking cotton bedsheets, passing behind her eyes. "I can't leave him alone. What should I do?"

What about old Mrs. Collins next door? She always says hello to Sam, maybe she'll pop over for 20 minutes. She is a bit odd, though, always in that same housedress, smelling like stale beer and wine and smoke, her eyes never meeting yours. Well, that's not *that* odd, Arla continued to argue with herself. She probably hasn't got any money for nice clothes, and she's probably shy. So she drinks a bit. It's only 20 minutes. Arla glanced at the clock. 11:30. Pretty late to be disturbing neighbours.

Arla crossed the hallway to Mrs. Collins' apartment and listened at the door. She heard the TV, saw light shining under the door, took a chance, and knocked. Mrs. Collins opened the door. The old woman's familiar smells and downcast eyes made Arla hesitate a moment, but she made her request. Okay, Mrs. Collins said, but could she have a little money for doing it? Yes, said Arla, and Mrs. Collins picked up the can of beer she'd been drinking and the *National Enquirer* she'd been reading, turned off the TV, and followed Arla to her door.

"Thanks so much," said Arla, as Mrs. Collins slid into the easy chair in Arla's living room and Arla headed for the door, shutting it quietly behind her, so as not to wake Sam.

It was a beautiful, clear night. A million stars, a slim crescent of moon, the wind light. Arla headed toward the lakeshore, walking briskly.

The lake was calm and black, part of the sky. In the dark the concrete path at the lake's edge bled into the grass; it might have been a dirt path, packed firm by horses' hooves. It might have been a hundred years ago, a time when things were more... organic? Is that the word? Healthier? Is that what she wanted? Is health something you find or something you create? Arla walked along the path, smelling grass and dirt, separating out chemical odours, tagging them for removal, putting them aside. Smelling only grass and dirt. She stretched her arms. Her muscles were tight. If I run a bit, I'll loosen up, she thought.

Arla began to run slowly, letting her muscles relax. She listened to herself think. People are a pain in the ass. The runner, Brian, the Buddhists, everybody. Hell is other people, Sartre said. But Sartre's not fashionable now. *Trouble with hating everyone is that you are everyone.* I don't hate Sam, that's about the only person I don't hate. This is not healthy. Something's going wrong with the way I think.

She began picking up speed. The wind pushed back her hair. She felt the tension leave her mouth and forehead. Her skin felt cool and smooth as polished amber. There was something about this running, all right. Just the wind, water, sky. She stopped thinking about people, about hating them. She didn't have to feel anything but the freedom of her body as it moved.

The legs circled easily on a bicycle of air. Feet hit the firm ground in a regular rhythm. The spine, the magical erect spine, defiant of gravity, aligned itself with the stars. The eyes filled with air, water, earth, and the glimmering spots of light in the darkness. Arms kept the beautiful motion going, kept it balanced. Breathing was smooth, unnoticed.

Arla was running at a steady pace now, muscles and bones working together. No one was around. Suddenly a car pulled up ahead, its lights flashing. She stopped. It was a police car. Two large policemen got out and came toward her.

"It's a little late for you to be out here by yourself, isn't it?" the taller one said. He was smooth-faced, broad-shouldered, and handsome in a bland way, like a high school football player. His face looked strained. For a moment Arla thought she recognized him as one of the players on her high school's team who had missed getting an athletic scholarship because his grades hadn't been high enough.

"Why, what time is it?" Arla asked.

"One in the morning."

"I didn't realize it was that late," she said. She felt dizzy and leaned against the railing that bordered the lake.

"Are you all right, lady?" The same cop did all the talking. The other just watched. "Maybe we should drive you home." He came over to her and extended his arm, supporting her by the elbow. "Would you like that, lady, a ride home?" He smiled slightly at her and moved his hand along her lower arm.

"Oh no, no. I'm fine. I have to get home. My little boy needs me," she said quickly. "But thanks just the same. Thanks." She withdrew her arm from his hand.

"Did you leave your kid alone, lady? That's child neglect," said the cop. He grasped her by the elbow again, but harder than before.

"You're hurting me," Arla said. He tightened his grip. He was pulling her toward the police car.

"Hey, Frank, forget it," said the quiet cop. "How do you know who she is?"

The tall cop stopped, but continued to hold Arla's arm. "Probably one of those welfare bums. Or a Parkdale hooker. Are you a hooker, lady?"

The cop's voice flashed hot in Arla's ears. Her lips

felt glued together, her legs like garden hoses just emptied of water.

"What's the matter with you, leaving your kid alone? This neighbourhood is really starting to stink. What it needs is a good cleaning out."

Arla tried to speak, to say Sam was with a neighbour, that she hadn't left him alone, but her stuck lips would not open; she was in a bad-dream paralysis. And that minute in time when she'd considered leaving Sam alone drummed around in her head; she deserved this.

The cop began pulling her toward the car again. She jerked back from him and tried to run. He held her arm and swung her around to face him, his mouth tight with anger. Arla waited for the other arm to let loose.

"Frank, I said *forget it*." The other cop's voice was nervous, irritated. "You don't know who she is. Anyway, I'm tired. Leave her alone. C'mon."

The tall cop stood still for a minute, held Arla's arm and looked at her. Then he let go of her arm. "Get out of here," he said. "Go home. And don't be out here any more at this time of night. Women shouldn't be out alone at this time of night. Go home and take care of your kid. Go on, *move*."

Arla walked backwards a few steps. Her rubber-hose legs began to bend.

"Get out of here, goddammit." The cop raised his voice, and took a step toward her. She turned around and walked slowly away from them. It took a long time to walk back home. The muscles which had moved so wondrously as she ran under the crescent moon now would not kick into gear. They belonged to someone else, someone who knew what a bad person Arla was, that hurrying her along would bring good to no one.

The small apartment building Arla lived in came into view and panic overtook her. What if Mrs. Collins had hurt Sam? What if she'd gotten tired of waiting, gone home, and left him alone? What if she'd kidnapped him? The world was an extremely dangerous place, how could Arla have left Sam with an oddball neighbour she scarcely knew? Who smelled of beer and wine and never changed her clothes? Arla's legs began to work and she ran the last half-block home, bursting through her apartment door out of breath.

Mrs. Collins sat snoring in the easy chair, the *National Enquirer* opened on her lap. Arla raced into Sam's room. He was sleeping soundly. She felt his head and it seemed like the fever might be gone. His breathing was a little lighter. How could she have left him with Mrs. Collins? What if something had happened to him? She would have died. "What's the matter with me? What's going on?" she said aloud.

Arla stroked Sam's cheek and hair and wiped some perspiration from his forehead with a corner of the blanket. She shook the blanket out, spreading it carefully back over him, tucking it in at his shoulders and feet. As she left the room, she felt her shirt wet on her breasts, from sweat, and her face streaming wet with tears. She roused Mrs. Collins, escorted her to the door, closed and locked it quietly after her.

Arla walked softly to the bedroom, lay down on her bed without undressing and fell into a deep sleep.

SEVEN

ARLA WOKE UP THE NEXT MORNING feeling rested. Light streamed through the curtains. She heard Sam in the next room, talking to his stuffed animals. He's feeling better and the sun's out, Arla thought. Things are back to normal. She turned on her side, leaned out of bed toward the telephone on the floor, and plugged it back into the jack. She lay back in bed and watched the shadows cast by maple leaves on the curtains.

Then she remembered the previous night. Thinking about it gave her a headache. She decided she was tired after all. It was a false feeling she'd felt at the moment of waking, that feeling of being rested. No, she was tired. She would go back to sleep for a while until Sam wanted her attention.

The phone rang. She leaned over to pull the cord out of the jack, changed her mind, and picked up the receiver. "Yes?" she said.

"Where the hell have you been? Are you all right?" It was Brian.

"We're okay. I had a bad week and unplugged the phone. I'm sorry," she said.

"Fucking right you should be sorry. What am I supposed to think? Don't you think I might have been worried? I mean just a little bit?" Brian's voice was high and fast.

"To tell you the truth, it never occurred to me you might be worried. If you were so worried, why didn't you come by?"

"You told me not to."

"I guess I did. But if you were really worried, you would have come by anyway," Arla said.

"I can't win with you, can I?"

"Brian, I'm not feeling well. Can I call you back in a few hours?"

"What's the matter?"

"I've got a really bad headache. Hardly got any sleep last night."

"Why? What were you doing?"

Arla paused before answering. "Nothing. I had insomnia. You know I have trouble sleeping."

"Mm-hmm." It was Brian's grunt of suspicion.

"What do you think I was doing?"

"I don't know. Your phone was unplugged all week. Maybe you were trying out some other guys. Need a little variety. I don't know."

Trying out some other guys. Some other guys were trying me out. "Some cops hassled me," she said.

"What?"

"I went for a walk by the lake last night. Some cops stopped me and threatened me. I got home late. I'm really upset about it. I wasn't doing anything, just taking a walk. It was really scary."

"Mm-hmm," Brian grunted.

"One of the cops tried to drag me to his car. He hurt my arm. Then the other cop told him to leave me alone and he did."

"C'mon, Arla, you can do better than that. That's pretty wild," Brian said.

Arla felt like throwing the phone through the window. Instead she said quietly, "Why should I make up a story like that? If I wanted to hide something from you, I'd go for a more boring story."

"Weren't you telling me that your redheaded friend told you a story about the cops?"

"Yes, I guess I did," Arla said. She had forgotten all about the runner's story about the cops at the lake.

"Sounds to me like you just lifted it. You would have done better to pick some story told by a sane person. Cops don't just go around beating up people. They lose their jobs for that kind of stuff."

Arla remembered saying something similar to the runner. Her headache was compressing her skull bones, making the blood pulsate.

"If you don't want to believe me, that's your problem. I don't feel well. I'm taking some aspirin and going back to sleep. Bye, Brian." Arla hung up the phone and pulled the cord out of the jack. She pulled the covers over her head and closed her eyes.

Someone was knocking at the door. "There's a goddamn fucking conspiracy against me," Arla said into the pillow and pulled it over her head. The knocking continued. "Goddamn it. Persistent son of a bitch." Arla kept muttering to herself. "If it's the runner or the Hydro collector, I'll pretend I'm not here." She walked quietly to the door in her bare feet and looked through the little hole. It was Felicia. Arla opened the door.

"Well, am I glad to see you," Felicia said. "We've been trying to call you. Nobody's been able to get you in. I was beginning to worry. Is Sam okay?"

"Yes, he's okay now. Just listen," Arla said, smiling a little. Sam was singing the alphabet song.

"I'm so glad. I heard he was sick and no one could get you and I worried, you know, that maybe he was very sick... I didn't know what to think, really. Here, I made these whole-wheat carrot muffins for you. All natural ingredients."

"Thanks, that's really nice... that's..." Arla began to cry.

"Hey, what's the matter? What's going on?"

Arla sat on the sofa and let herself cry. Felicia sat next to her with one hand on Arla's shoulder and one hand clutching the bag of carrot muffins. Arla cried for a while. When she finally stopped, she wiped her eyes with the back of her hand.

"What's wrong, Arla?" Felicia asked.

"I don't know. I'm not feeling well. I had a terrible week, Felicia. And I had a terrible night, last night."

"What happened?" Felicia asked.

"What happened?" Arla repeated Felicia's words and sat back against the sofa, rubbing her forehead and saying nothing.

"Hey, Arla, talk to me. This isn't very useful," Felicia said.

"I had a bad dream, a horrible nightmare," Arla said. "It made me very upset. I can't get it out of my mind. I don't know what it means."

"What did you dream?" Felicia brightened up. Dreams and visions were her favourite subjects.

"I dreamt I left Sam with a crazy neighbour, and went down to the lake. I started running. I was running very fast and feeling good. Then some cops pulled up in a car. They threatened me. One of them started pulling me toward his car. I thought he was going to force me into his car and beat me up. I was scared. I still feel scared, really scared. And this morning when I woke up, I remembered that the dream is like a story my friend, you know, the one who watches Sam sometimes, it's like a story she told me about something that happened to her."

"Well, that's what the dream means," Felicia said cheerfully. "She's gone."

"What do you mean?" Arla asked. She thought she was going to be sick.

"She just disappeared. She'd been coming every day to the drop-in and then she didn't come for a few days, so a couple of people went to look for her. She wasn't home and they couldn't find her anywhere. The baby was there, though. She'd left him by himself."

"Oh no. Was he all right?"

"Children's Aid has him. He was nearly dehydrated. But they found him in time. Looks like he's going to be okay."

"Oh my god," said Arla.

"There's something else. I wasn't going to tell you, but the police will be asking questions, so they might say something to you."

"The last thing I want to do now is talk to cops."

"Well, I don't know if they will come around here or not. Don't worry about it. They're just asking people routine questions. But they'll probably be here, because she left a shopping bag with your name and address on it, which is what I want to tell you about. I think it will be better if you hear it from me."

"So tell me."

"Well, it had Sam's clothes and things in it. I guess

you left a few things there for when she took care of him,"
Felicia said.

"So?"

"Okay, well, don't get upset, but the clothes were all
ripped up. I mean, they weren't in pieces, but she, or
someone, but it must have been her, had taken scissors
and cut long slits all over them."

"Oh christ," Arla said. "Why would she do that?
What could she have against Sam?"

"Don't try to figure it out. She's sick, she's not
rational."

"It must have been a way to get at me," Arla said.
"She must have been mad that I stayed in all week and
didn't let her follow me around everywhere like she was
doing before. And she must have been mad about the
evening with Brian."

"Just be glad she wasn't taking care of Sam when she
was mad at you," Felicia said.

Arla looked at Felicia and they were both quiet for a
minute. "Oh christ," Arla said again. She put her hand
over her mouth, rushed to the bathroom and threw up
in the toilet. Felicia came after her.

"Are you all right?"

"I think so," Arla said, leaning back against the sink.

"Pretty scary to think of her taking care of Sam,"
Felicia said.

Arla ran the tap, rinsed her mouth, and washed her
face. She filled a glass with water and drank it slowly while

she sat on the toilet. Then the two women walked back to the living room. Arla looked out the window, and repressed a desire to close the curtains. Not a healthy thing to do in the middle of the morning on a bright August day. "I should never have left him with her. I haven't been thinking carefully. Something's been going wrong with the way I think," Arla said.

"You're just upset and I don't blame you. You've been in all week. Sam's been sick. You had a bad dream, and here I come with this news. Take it easy, you're okay, there's nothing wrong with you."

"Well, there's something wrong with the world. The runner was right about how bad things are. She's part of what's going wrong with the universe. I'm part of it, too, part of its disease. You're part of what's okay with the universe, part of its health."

"Listen, big speeches about the universe are *my* specialty. Don't be so dramatic. It's been a bad week. It's over. Everything's all right now. Take it easy. You're *okay*. Sam's okay. We're all okay."

"Maybe so, I hope so."

Felicia was staring at the big canvas propped against the wall. "So you finally got a start on those self-portraits you were having so much trouble with," she said.

"That's not me, Felicia." Arla's stomach felt sick again.

"It looks pretty much like you. Except for the red

hair. The expressions are a little strange, too. You don't usually do that with your mouth," Felicia said.

Arla looked at the painting. Felicia was right. The portraits did look like her: She thought she was painting the runner and had wound up painting herself, or herself with the hair and expressions of the runner. The runner was taking her over. Now, looking at the painting, it was so clear. How could she have missed seeing it all this time? Her headache had broken up into small sharp pains all over her head: they darted about under her scalp, minnows in shallow water. "I think I'd like to be alone a while," she said to Felicia. "Do you mind?"

"I'm not sure you should be alone. You're pretty upset," Felicia said.

Arla took a deep breath. "No, I'm okay now. I'm going to have some tea and one of your muffins and work on this painting."

"Are you sure?"

"Yes, really. I'll call you later. Thanks for coming by. You're a good friend, you know that, don't you?" Arla said.

"All right. If you don't call me, I'll call you. Don't unplug your phone today," Felicia said. She leaned over and kissed Arla on the cheek.

"Here, see, I'm plugging the phone in," Arla said.

"Talk to you later," Felicia said and went out the door.

Arla watched Felicia through the window, waiting until she had rounded the corner. She went to the kitchen, took a large pair of scissors out of the drawer, and felt its sharpness with her thumb. She walked over to the big canvas and without pausing drew the scissors up and down against it, making numerous long, smooth incisions. Almost time for the morning pick-up. She carried the canvas out back to the trash bins.

Arla went back inside, sat down with her drawing pad, and began sketching her own face. I'll do some studies and start those self-portraits again, she thought. I'll do myself on purpose this time. She propped a small mirror against the lamp on the table and looked at her reflection.

The eyes are always the hardest part to do, she thought. Maybe that's why the runner's ex-husband did her mouth in that painting on her wall. Arla picked up the mirror and looked at her face closely, noting, as she had done in the past, that the whole face is reflected in the pupil. It's hard to get that on canvas without it looking forced, she thought. Also, when you do that, it's difficult to get the look, the glance outward, the eyes as a whole. It's hard to get both things at once on the canvas. Why did the runner have such a hard time looking people in the eyes? Maybe when she looked all she could see was herself. The runner wasn't right about everything. But she was right about some things. The trick is to figure it out each time, to make judgements about everything, one piece at a time. To try and see each thing clearly.

I have to call Felicia tomorrow and tell her what happened down at the lake was no dream. And we ought to look for the runner. We ought to find out what happened, exactly. Arla turned her eyes back to the drawing pad and continued sketching.